"I came to Widow's Peak Creek to learn why my mom never spoke of her past."

Vindication flooded his veins, hot and triumphant. "I was right. You held back from me."

"Yes, but it's not what you think. I'm not here for the inheritance." She met his gaze squarely. "I'm searching for my father."

The cable slipped between his fingers. "What? You don't have any idea who your father is?"

"My birth certificate is blank under 'Father,' and my mom refuses to discuss the topic. It's eaten me up inside. For years." Harper's eyes were tearless but drowning in agony all the same. "This is such a mess. All I wanted was to know who I am."

Joel let out a long, slow breath.

That look in her eyes? He'd seen it a hundred times in the mirror after Adriana died. Reflecting his pain. His uncertainty. His need for God's strength to carry on. That look couldn't be faked. Not even by award-winning actors.

She was telling the truth, wasn't she?

Susanne Dietze began writing love stories in high school, casting her friends in the starring roles. Today, she's an award-winning, RWA RITA® Award–nominated author who's seen her work on the ECPA and *Publishers Weekly* bestseller lists for inspirational fiction. Married to a pastor and the mom of two, Susanne lives in California and enjoys fancy-schmancy tea parties, the beach and curling up on the couch with a costume drama. To learn more, say hi or sign up for her newsletter, visit her website, www.susannedietze.com.

Books by Susanne Dietze

Love Inspired

Widow's Peak Creek

Love Inspired Historical

Visit the Author Profile page at LoveInspired.com.

The Secret Between Them

Susanne Dietze

LOVE INSPIRED
INSPIRATIONAL ROMANCE

LOVE INSPIRED®

INSPIRATIONAL ROMANCE

ISBN-13: 978-1-335-58594-3

The Secret Between Them

This is a work of fiction. Names, characters, places and incidents are either the
product of the author's imagination or are used fictitiously. Any resemblance
to actual persons, living or dead, businesses, companies, events or locales is
entirely coincidental.

For questions and comments about the quality of this book, please contact us
at CustomerService@Harlequin.com.

Love Inspired
22 Adelaide St. West, 41st Floor
Toronto, Ontario M5H 4E3, Canada
www.LoveInspired.com

Printed in U.S.A.

But I am like a green olive tree
in the house of God: I trust in the mercy of God
for ever and ever.
—*Psalm* 52:8

To the Garlic Knots—
Ashley, Emma, Hannah S., Hannah T.,
Megan and my Hannah D. Your camaraderie
and love for Jesus fill my heart with joy. Thanks
for your prayers and for the fabulous illustrated
notes some of you made for me (including Joseph,
not a Knot but married to one!).
I will treasure them always.

Acknowledgments

Many thanks to John Copeland and
Shannon Casey of Rancho Olivos in Santa Ynez,
California, who graciously answered my questions
about olives, oil and life among their beautiful
trees. The photos and explanations were so
helpful, but I claim responsibility for any errors
in the story. Thank you, cousin!

I'm also grateful to those who prayed for me
and with me as I finished this book.

Chapter One

Joel Morgan was not in the mood to be lied to.

Folding his arms over his chest, he stared down the strawberry blonde who'd just burst through the door of Price & Morgan, Widow's Peak Creek's sole firm specializing in family law. "May I see some ID, please?"

"Excuse me?" Her brown eyes shot sparks of fire. "Last I heard, a person didn't have to provide proof of identification to speak to a lawyer. Or a family member."

If she were indeed a family member of Joel's mentor, Clark Price. A little piece of plastic wouldn't completely prove she was Clark's granddaughter, but it could sure disprove it, fast. And no way was he giving this stranger a scrap of information until he'd seen her name and picture on something official. "I can't be of any help to you unless I see a government-issued photo ID."

Joel leaned against the heavy reception desk in the firm's lobby. The space had once been the foyer of the Victorian-era home, but a few decades ago, the house had transitioned to a place of business. The dark wood and sophisticated furnishings were expensive, the sort that usually impressed clients and intimidated opposing counsel.

The surroundings didn't seem to have any effect on the strawberry blonde, though. She waited as if expecting him to retract his request for identification, her freckled nose and chin tipped up at an angle that said she was offended.

If he was rude, well, so be it. He'd run out of patience with conniving liars about an hour ago.

Muttering, she dug into the tan leather satchel dangling over her left forearm and pulled out a thin black wallet. "Maybe I should ask for your ID, too. I have no idea who you are, and you sure don't look like you work in a law office."

In his untucked button-down, jeans and boots, he had to admit she had a point. "Casual Friday." Even though he dressed like this pretty much every day unless he was in court. He kept a few ties in a drawer in his office, however. Just in case.

But she was right about his failure to introduce himself. "I'm the Morgan of Price & Morgan. Joel."

The once-thriving legal office now only employed two others beside him. The administrative assistant, Shirley, and Tammy, a part-time paralegal, had already left work for the weekend since the office closed at noon on Fridays in the summer. Joel had stayed on after lunch today to get more work done, grateful for the quiet he only found when he was in the office alone.

Alone until she'd come in, that is—the woman with her hair clipped up in one of those bun-ponytail styles he could never achieve when he helped his stepdaughter, Maisie, with her hair.

"Here." She slapped a plastic rectangle on the reception desk. "Proof I am who I say I am."

Not so fast. Joel gave the Arizona driver's license a thorough look over.

Harper R. Price. Her name checked out, and so did the birthdate, twenty-nine years ago. He was no expert on forged IDs, but this looked legitimate.

Fine. She was Clark's granddaughter.

But that didn't mean she wasn't lying about a host of other things.

He handed back her license. "Why don't we step into my office?"

"I'd rather be shown to my grandfather's office." Nevertheless, she followed the direction of Joel's gesture, striding into the room he indicated to the right of the lobby. "I've come a long way to see him."

A pang hit Joel in the chest. For Clark's sake, he wished Harper Price had made the trek a long time ago. Other than a brief letter from Harper's mother, Sheila, written right after Harper was born, there had been no contact between them.

Clark had tried to remedy that. He sent Sheila letter after letter, but since Joel joined the firm, each of the letters Clark mailed to her had all come back unopened, marked "Return to Sender."

Clark had made light of it, singing the old Elvis Presley song by the same name whenever the mail came back to him. Despite the peppy tune, though, Joel had known how grieved his beloved mentor was by Sheila's refusal to reconcile.

And, by extension, Harper's refusal, too.

Now it was too late for a family reunion. Clark had passed nine months ago, and on two occasions since then, Joel had mailed letters from the law firm to the address on the internet that was linked to Sheila in Arizona. Neither letter had returned with one of those yellow stickers from the postal service indicating the addressee had moved. That had to mean Sheila had received them, and presumably Harper knew about them too.

Clark was the kindest, most honorable man Joel had ever known, and Sheila's and Harper's callous treatment toward him broke Joel's heart and hardened it at the same time. Hardened it so much, in fact, that if he had his way, he'd give Harper a few choice words and send her back to Arizona.

A quick glance at the black-framed photo propped on his desk stopped him, though. His stepdaughter, Maisie, freckled and missing her two front teeth, grinned out at him from the recent photograph. She might not be his daughter legally—not yet—but in every other way, Joel was her dad. She was the joy of his life.

And he owed it all to Clark. Joel never would have come to Widow's Peak Creek if Clark hadn't seen his potential and hired him. Joel wouldn't have received Clark's mentoring in both his profession and his faith. Nor would Joel have met his wife, Adriana, when Maisie was just an infant. Clark had been the best man at Joel's wedding to Adriana.

And without Clark's support when Adriana died two years ago, Joel might not have made it through.

So Joel would do what Clark asked of him, even though he had no desire to have this conversation with Harper. Joel was bound, legally and out of friendship, to do it.

"Please take a seat." He gestured at one of the black leather chairs set in front of his desk. "We have a lot to discuss."

"*We?* I'm here to see my grandfather, not—"

Harper broke off, her hand going to her chest in a gesture of shock. "He's gone, isn't he?"

As if she didn't know. Why was she pretending this was a surprise?

Joel didn't feel like prolonging their talk by challenging this charade of hers, though. "Cancer."

She sank into the chair then. The way she moved, with her head tilted to the right, struck him as familiar. It made sense that her actions should be recognizable, though, if she were Clark's granddaughter.

"I'm so sorry." She shut her eyes for a moment.

"Me too." Joel bit back a retort that if she'd cared, she would've come when Clark was alive. Instead, he reached into a drawer for a manila file. "As the executor of his estate, I've been entrusted with informing you and your mother of his wishes. Is she in town with you?"

Harper flinched. "She doesn't even know I'm in California."

"You should inform her, then, and have her join you. There's a time limit to take into consideration."

"She's halfway across the world—did you say 'time limit'?" Her head jerked up in surprise. "You mean he just passed away? There hasn't been a funeral yet?"

"That's not what I meant. The funeral was held a week after he died. Nine months ago." Joel shoved down his irritation over the fact that she continued to feign ignorance. "I'm talking about the inheritance."

"The what?"

She was a decent actress, he'd give her that. Her shock almost looked and sounded real.

"You and your mother were given one year to claim what Clark left for you. Otherwise, his instructions were to donate his estate to charity. Considering three-quarters of that year have passed, that leaves three months for you and your mother to sign the paperwork, so you might want to ask her to hurry."

"She's on a culinary cruise in the Mediterranean right now." She bent forward, staring at the rug.

"Last I checked, people can receive text messages and emails at sea. Phone calls, too. Don't you think her father's death is worth disrupting her cruise?" His tone was a touch sarcastic, but Sheila had probably timed her vacation to coincide with Harper's visit to sniff out the inheritance. She was probably sunning herself on the pool deck, more concerned with her tan than her father's passing.

"Of course, but I don't want to deliver that sort of news in an email or text. Maybe I'm not thinking clearly, but I'd feel better about telling her over the phone when she disembarks in a few weeks." She rubbed her forehead. "I can tell you disapprove, but like I said, she doesn't even know I'm here. Things are…complicated."

His hand fisted, and he forced it to flex. He mustn't give in to his frustration. The fastest way through this was to forge ahead.

"Then whenever it's…convenient for you to speak to your mother, have her contact me. We can handle the matter of your inheritance right now, though. Clark left you property. An olive grove. Six hundred trees, give or take, planted over eight acres. Some of the trees date back to the gold rush era, but they're still producing." He pushed a packet across the desktop to her. "The details are in here."

"A grove?" Confusion marred her smooth features. "Why?"

What did she mean, why? Because Clark had wanted to give it to her.

Unless…she was asking why her grandfather hadn't left her something else—something flashier or liquid assets. The grove had worth, but if her mind had been set on inheriting jewelry or cash, it made sense that she'd be disappointed.

Too bad. He'd already encountered two other people today who wanted easy money. Not Clark's, of course, but his precious Maisie's.

Just thinking about it again made him want to hit the gym and spend a half hour with the punching bag. Somehow, someone in town had learned about his stepdaughter's inheritance and told a friend or two, because it had become a full-fledged rumor. He'd found out that morning, when he realized he'd forgotten a file on his desk at home and returned for it. Maisie's new nanny, Kjersti, had been on the phone, brainstorming ideas to "step up her plan" to get Joel to marry her. He'd been so sure he'd heard wrong he felt embarrassed confronting her.

He didn't feel embarrassed once Kjersti admitted what she'd heard about Maisie's money, which she'd assumed Joel controlled and could share with a new wife.

Firing her had been easy, but it created a few problems—like dealing with childcare for the rest of the summer. Friends had pitched in that morning, which was a blessing, and he trusted God would provide for the long term.

He wasn't sure how, though. Not just on the childcare front but with Maisie herself.

If the morning with Kjersti hadn't gone bad

enough, it had turned disastrous once he got to the office. He'd been trying to adopt Maisie for a few months now. All he needed was the consent of her wayward, gambling biological dad, Sebastian. A man who'd never even met her. But that morning, Joel had received an email from Sebastian's lawyer stating that Sebastian wished to contest the adoption.

Not only that, Sebastian intended to pursue full custody.

Joel grew hot just thinking about it again, as if his blood was boiling. The timing of Sebastian's sudden desire to be in Maisie's life couldn't be coincidental, coming on the heels of that rumor about Maisie's inheritance. Sebastian's aunt still lived in town, and she must have heard the story.

Regardless, Sebastian didn't want custody of Maisie, Joel was sure. Sebastian wanted custody—control—of her money.

Harper Price was no different than Sebastian or Kjersti. She was here because she wanted her inheritance from Clark, a man she had never cared about.

Throughout Joel's life, it seemed God had placed him in situations where he played the role of protector. This was one of those times, when it came to raising Maisie, and it was also appropriate when it came to Clark's legacy. He'd been entrusted to guard it.

His heart hardened a little more as he stared Harper down. "An olive grove. Take it or leave it."

Joel sure hoped she'd leave it—and Widow's Peak Creek, while she was at it. Clark Price deserved a lot better than a gold digger for a granddaughter.

An olive grove.

Harper, frankly, had hoped for something altogether different from her grandfather.

Like answers.

A wave of weariness washed over her. Emotional fatigue but physical, too. She'd been in the car for twelve hours, driving here to the Sierra Nevada foothills in Northern California from Phoenix. She'd braced herself to be rejected by Clark Price, certain he wouldn't welcome her since he'd rejected her mother thirty years ago.

But at least she would have seen him. Received context about why he and her mom had fallen out thirty years ago.

Lord, what am I to do now?

The white noise of the air conditioner's hiss would normally help her concentrate, but her brain was numb. Meanwhile, Joel Morgan was probably waiting for her to speak. What had he said? *Take it or leave it?*

Was that a bad attempt at a joke, or was he just impolite in general?

She decided to give him the benefit of the doubt. "My grandfather had a farm? Or grove, I mean? According to his bio on the website, he's still practicing law. Or was, before he passed away."

Maybe Joel would take the hint and update the firm's website.

"Lawyers are allowed to have hobbies, you know."

You couldn't judge a book by its cover, but the way Joel looked, she'd guess his hobbies included rugby and weightlifting. Over six feet tall and broad, the guy's muscular build was the sort that drew attention. His swooshy dark hair and chiseled features were a Hollywood actor's dream.

However, she wasn't the sort of person who was impressed—or daunted—by looks or size. She might be a full foot shorter than Joel Morgan, Esquire, or whatever he was called as a lawyer, but she wasn't intimidated by him or his curt demeanor.

And she wanted as much information about Clark Price as she could get. "So my grandfather's hobby was olives?"

"Not olives, exactly. But he enjoyed strolling through the grove from time to time. He bought the property ten years or so ago, added to the existing trees and found it to be a peaceful place to unwind."

"He wasn't hands-on with the trees?"

"He employed a farm manager, who is being paid for through the end of the year by a separate account. So you don't owe anything there, if that's what you're asking."

Wow, this guy was a piece of work, implying that she was only concerned with money. He clearly didn't like her.

He didn't have to like her, though. Their business would be finished soon enough. In the meantime, she'd get as much information about her grandfather from him as she could.

"That was not what I was asking. I wondered what he liked about it," she continued. "I wonder a lot of things because my grandfather is a complete unknown to me. Since you worked with him, would you mind telling me a little bit about him?"

"If you were truly curious about your grandfather, you would have come while he was alive, not waited until you'd inherited something from him."

She shifted deeper into the chair as if his words physically shoved her back. "I didn't know I had a grandfather until two days ago—or that he'd died until you told me."

"As a matter of point, I didn't tell you he died."

He might not look like a lawyer, but he sounded like one right now. She stifled the urge to roll her eyes. "It wasn't hard to figure out when you asked me to be seated in that all-business tone. But how could I have known he'd died when I didn't even know his name?"

He rubbed his temple. "As I wrote in the letters I sent to you, the grove is yours, so you can drop the pretense."

Pretense? "We didn't get any letters from you."

He didn't believe her. She could see it in his eyes.

She owed him nothing, but her chest tightened with the need to defend herself. "Look, I moved back in with my mom fourteen months ago, and I'm the one who brings in the mail every day. It comes right before I get home from work. If there were any letters from a law firm in California, I'd have seen them."

"You honestly expect me to believe both of them just happened to be stolen or lost?"

"I don't care what you believe, but it's the truth. I never saw them. Okay, listen—it's none of your business, but two days ago I stumbled across an old letter in a box of memorabilia.

My mom wrote it when she was pregnant with me but never mailed it. In it, she refers to her father, Clark Price, and the name of this town. That's the first I heard of either of them. An online search took me straight to this law firm's outdated website, so when I came today? I expected to find Clark. Alive."

Joel's expression didn't change. "Why didn't you call ahead to speak with him?"

"I wanted to see his face when he realized who I was." It sounded petulant, but it was true. "And I didn't want to run the risk that he'd turn me away. Clearly, things were complicated between him and my mother."

"That wasn't Clark's fault. He's tried reaching out for years now. Each letter he mailed to her was returned to sender. I saw those letters myself before he tossed them into the recycling bin, so no, I don't believe that he never came up in conversation between you two."

"My mother told me she didn't have any family."

"That was a lie, wasn't it?"

He was right. Her mom had lied. But she'd had it up to her steaming-hot earlobes with this guy's attitude.

"She had to have had a reason. I can't give you an explanation for why my mom didn't tell me anything, but I sure hoped I'd get an explanation myself today. My mother left this town thirty years ago as an unwed, pregnant young adult and never mentioned it again because clearly, her father and the people of this tiny town turned their backs on her. I came because she won't tell me why, and the obvious place to start was with my grandfather."

A muscle clenched in his jaw. "This *tiny town* is the warmest, most caring community I've ever been blessed to live in, and Clark was a good man. I don't take kindly to either being insulted."

Joel was sure taking this personally. "I can tell by the name of this law firm that he was your partner—"

"More than that. Clark was like family to me."

Harper wished it didn't sting that Clark had replaced her mother so handily. She and her mom had only had each other, and as often as they'd moved, it was sometimes lonely.

But it had been safe. They hadn't been hurt by anyone the way her mom must have been hurt by Clark. Joel might have found him to be a good man, but something didn't add up.

She let out a sigh. She had more questions than answers now. And she wasn't getting much information from Joel "Zip-Lip" Morgan. "I guess we're finished here, then."

The office's outer door creaked open. "Daddy?"

"In here, Bug." His grumpy expression giving way to a tender smile, Joel stood up and stepped around his desk. A tiny girl in a yellow sundress and pink-rimmed eyeglasses rushed inside, arms outstretched. He enveloped her in his enormous arms, swinging her up and setting her reddish-blond ponytail bouncing. She was such a dainty child she didn't look like she belonged to a dark-headed hulk of a man like him.

"Oh, I am so sorry." A pretty woman with long golden hair cringed as she lurked in the doorway. "I didn't realize you were with a client, Joel."

Harper wanted to snap that she was no client of Joel Morgan's, but this woman—his wife, probably—didn't deserve her waspish tongue. "No worries. We're finished."

Joel set his little girl down and smiled at the woman. "Thanks for keeping Maisie, Clementine."

"Our pleasure. Let me know if you need me to keep her again. I know what it's like being the only parent when childcare falls through. Anyway, I'm sorry for barging in." She slipped out with an apologetic smile for Harper that seemed to say she understood what happened in law offices was confidential, and she respected that.

Clearly this Clementine wasn't his wife after all. A quick glance revealed Joel did not wear

a wedding ring, and Clementine had implied
Joel was on his own as a parent. No matter how
cool Joel had been with her, her heart panged
for him and his little girl. When she was growing up, she'd learned the lot of a solitary parent
wasn't easy.

She wished him and his Maisie the best, but it
was time to part ways. She would find a motel,
get a good night's rest and then—

She had no idea what she'd do. Nothing today
had gone according to plan. But her short time
in Widow's Peak Creek would bear fruit somehow. God would help her.

*Right, Lord? Or is there no one left alive in
this town who can tell me who I am?*

Chapter Two

Harper scooped up the packet on Joel's desk. Maybe she'd find a nugget of information about her family among the olive grove paperwork. Any tidbit on Clark could be a clue into her mom's history.

One thing, though, before she left. Well, two things. "Is there anyone named Harper in town?"

"There's a Harper in my class at school," the little girl announced.

She smiled at her helpfulness. "Anyone older than me? Or a family with the surname of Harper?"

"Not that I know of." A wrinkle of confusion furrowed Joel's forehead. "Why?"

"My mom said I was named for someone kind, that's all, and I wondered who it was. Never mind." She waved the manila envelope, which felt heavier than she'd expected. Its weight reminded her of the second question she had. She'd never been left a legacy in someone's will, and she had no idea what she was supposed to do. "What's the protocol for this sort of thing? Am I allowed to go look at the olive grove?"

Nodding, Joel lifted a black bag up by the strap, signaling he was leaving the office, too. "The land is yours to do with as you please."

She peeked into the envelope. A brass key among a thick stack of paperwork explained the weight. "I assume it's got an address I can find on my phone? It isn't in the boonies with no cell reception, is it?"

"What's a boonie?" The little girl eyed Joel sideways. Harper had to take a second look because the girl's left eye didn't quite track with the right.

"It means a place out in the middle of nowhere." Joel winked at his daughter. "And no, it's not far at all. If you're interested in going there now, you can follow us. We live on the adjoining property."

Neighbors, eh? It didn't look like Harper was done with Joel Morgan quite yet after all. Not unless the properties were separated by a high, thick fence.

Thankfully, her finicky car started right up, and she was able to pull out into the street directly behind the Morgans' charcoal gray F-150. Joel drove the speed limit, as if he had precious cargo in the back seat or was conscious that he was being followed by a newcomer to town.

Either way, she appreciated his efforts. The slower pace allowed her to take note of street signs and pretty scenery as they passed through a neighborhood of quaint Craftsman-style homes. They crossed a short bridge over the creek that gave the town its name, and the trees thinned as they veered north, allowing her full view of the Sierra Nevada. The properties grew larger, and quick glimpses off the roadside revealed crops and livestock—were those white balls of fluff she just passed a flock of sheep? That wasn't something she saw too often.

Within ten minutes of leaving the law office, Joel's turn signal indicator came on, and she followed him onto a long driveway bisecting a grove of slender olive trees, their silvery-green leaves fluttering in the summer breeze. Joel parked in front of a modular house that reminded her of the miniature cabins she made as a child out of Lincoln Logs—full of character but more fitting in a mountain setting.

Joel had said nothing about a house, just a grove. Maybe the grove was for Harper and the house was her mother's inheritance.

She parked behind him, cracked her windows to keep the interior from baking in the heat and got out. "Thanks for leading me here."

"No problem. Like I said, we live next door."

She raked her gaze over the property. To the right behind the house, a weathered brown barn looked neglected. So did the plot of land on the other side of the house, where nothing grew but scraggly weeds. Perhaps her grandfather had intended to build a permanent structure on it or planned a large yard for entertaining but never got around to it.

Olive trees had been planted on the rest of the property. Without flowers blooming in front of the porch or lawn or decorative shrubs, there was no splash of color other than the grass-green gate in the wood-slat fence dividing the property from the neighbors' place.

She glanced at Joel. "My grandfather doesn't seem to have been the decorating type."

"He didn't live here. His home was sold off right away, per his wishes. This house came with the place when he bought it, and he offered it to visiting missionaries, that sort of thing. It's furnished, but no one's been here for a while. The utilities were shut off months ago. Anyway, it's yours now."

"I thought maybe the house was for my mom and the trees were for me."

"The house is part of the property he designated for you. He had something else in mind for your mother." His attention fixed on his daughter, who'd run up to the porch. She crouched and peered at something at her feet. "What do you see, Bug?"

"Ants. They're going up the steps."

Harper smiled. She used to do the same sort of thing as a kid—study insects. Ants and bees had been her favorites because they were so industrious.

"Are they going to the house or away from it?" Joel's boots clomped up the steps.

"Neither. They're on the porch so they can visit in the shade, I think."

What a cutie, making up a story for the ants. In truth, Harper suspected that the ants might be interested in water on such a warm day, although she would've thought they'd manage among the irrigated olive trees. Or maybe, like her, they wanted shelter for the night. Her choice was one of the motels by the interstate, however—not a house without power or water.

"We haven't met officially." Harper smiled at the little girl. "I'm Harper. Your name's Maisie?"

"Maisie Jane Davis but it's gonna be Morgan soon. Maisie Jane Davis Morgan."

What did that mean? Maisie wasn't Joel's? Well, that explained why they looked so different from one another, but it begat several questions that were none of Harper's business. "That's a nice name, Maisie Jane."

"Daddy and I live over there with Fluff." Maisie hopped off the porch, pointing to the green gate in the fence.

"Fluff? Is that a cat?"

Maisie's tiny fist went to her hip. "He's a rabbit and softer than anything. Softer than a cotton ball."

"Wow, that's soft." Harper glanced at the treetops visible over their mutual fence. "Looks like you grow olives at your place, too."

"Olives, pomegranates, English walnuts, a few Meyer lemons, but they're not mine. We live in the guest house," Joel said just as a woman in her late fifties with bobbed auburn curls came through the gate. "She's the property owner."

The woman hurried toward them on a path skirting the trees. "You must be Harper Price." She extended her hand. "Joel called me from his car to tell me you were coming. I'm Trish Davis, your next-door neighbor. I understand Clark was your grandpa. I didn't know your mother, except by sight, but your grandpa was such a dear fellow. So what do you think of our town?"

"It's beautiful." But that didn't mean Harper was inclined to like Widow's Peak Creek. Not after her mother had felt no recourse but to flee this town. And she didn't quite buy that Clark was so "dear," although Trish certainly seemed to think so.

Trish's wide smile revealed a tiny speck of red lipstick on her front teeth. "I think it's the prettiest place in the world, but I'm biased. My family has been here forever. And by forever, I mean since the town's founding a hundred and seventy years ago."

Joel glanced at Harper. "Trish's passion is genealogy."

"*One* of my passions. I have a few." Trish pushed her black hipster glasses high up onto her nose. "My trees, of course. My work. I run a gourmet-food store downtown, and I also enjoy spending time with my great niece here."

Harper had assumed that Trish was Joel's landlord. "I didn't realize you're related."

"Trish is my late wife's aunt," Joel clarified.

Oh. That explained the comment about him parenting alone. He might be a grouch, but that didn't mean she was without compassion for him and Maisie. Before she could respond with a word of sympathy, however, Trish clicked her tongue. "Do you know much about olives, Harper?"

"Eating, yes, but growing? Not a thing. I'm a pastry chef. I didn't even know olives grew in this part of California."

"Oh, yes." Trish nodded sagely. "There are olive trees in Widow's Peak Creek that are over a hundred and fifty years old, brought by the forty-niners during the gold rush. Olives live a long time, you know."

Joel had said something to that effect, but Harper's brain returned to something else Joel had said before the mention of his wife's passing. Genealogy.

Family trees and documents and all that sort of thing—just what Harper needed help with. After all, answers were the main reason she'd come to Widow's Peak Creek.

Sure, she'd wanted to meet her grandfather and come to understand why her mom left town. But even more, she was desperate to find out the answer to the one question that had plagued her for almost all her twenty-nine years of life.

Who was her father?

Her mom had always given her the same answer: *Just someone it turned out I didn't know as well as I thought I did. But it's okay. We're the perfect family as we are, the two of us.*

The not knowing was like an itch inside her, though. Impossible to scratch but also impossible to ignore.

The urge to ask Trish for guidance with genealogy burned her tongue like an acid-sour candy, but she had to be patient and wait for the right time. This was not the sort of topic she could bring up in front of a little girl—

An ear-piercing shriek rent the air—loud,

unhuman and so unexpected it stole Harper's breath and sent her jumping out of her skin.

Straight into Joel's massive chest.

No woman had been this close to Joel since Adriana died, and it didn't seem right that it was a money-hungry liar like Harper Price who now clutched his shirtfront in both fists.

He should step back, but he caught himself patting her back. Gold digger or not, she trembled like a quaking aspen. "It's all right. It's just Beau."

She twisted her head, looking for the source of the noise. "But what's a Beau?"

"It's short for *bee-yoo-tiful*, even though they don't sound the same. B-yoo, Bo. Anyway, he's over there." Maisie tugged Harper out of Joel's arms and pointed at the grove.

Now that his arms were free, Joel could breathe easier, find the humor in the situation as emotions paraded across Harper's delicate features. From uncertainty to puzzlement, then shock, followed by the pink-tinged flush of embarrassment as she realized the loud noise that had scared her out of her wits had come from a bright blue bird a little smaller than a turkey, walking through the grove, parallel to the house, his tail fan trailing behind him.

Her face relaxed into a wide smile. "A peacock? I may not know much about Widow's Peak Creek, but I'm positive peafowl are not native birds."

"Oh, no." Trish shook her head. "Someone must have tried to keep a pair as pets, and they either escaped or were encouraged to, if you get my drift. Anyway, there's a pride of them now—that's what a group of them is called, or an ostentation. An apt name for a bird known as a show-off. They showed up in the neighborhood a couple of years ago—the same week Maisie and Joel moved into my guest house."

Joel remembered it well. He'd needed a change of scenery after Adriana died of a heart defect, so he'd taken Trish up on her offer to stay in the guest house on her property. He'd pulled his car into Trish's driveway, and there was Beau, strutting between Trish's lemon trees. Maisie had been delighted.

He'd always be grateful to Trish for helping them out in that way. Grateful that she was family.

Not that Harper or her mom would understand that, the way they'd ignored Clark.

"Beau just roams free, then?" Harper watched the peacock as he kept going past, his vibrant blue crest wobbling with each step.

"He only does what he wants to do," Maisie said. "Sometimes I want him to fan his tail and look pretty, but he just won't, no matter how nicely I ask."

Joel held back a snort. Sometimes Maisie's "pretty-pleases" with the bird were demands, not requests. "Beau's an independent guy. Peacocks get lonely by themselves, according to what I've learned on the internet, but my best guess is he's not the dominant male, so he comes exploring around our houses every so often." Not that it would affect Harper in any way since she wasn't going to stay. "Anyway, he does his own thing and takes care of himself."

Trish chuckled. "He's a good pest manager."

Maisie pointed at the porch. "Beau, come eat these ants."

"I'm not sure I want to be in his way if that happens." Harper pulled a face of mock fear. "I ought to look inside the house, anyway. Nice to meet you, Trish."

"Same, Harper. Don't be a stranger, now."

Trish was being polite, but as far as Joel was concerned, the sooner Harper left town, the better. To that end, he had a little more to discuss with her, and there was no time like the present. "Trish, would you mind hanging out with Maisie for a minute?"

"Say no more. Come on, Maisie. I need help picking tomatoes."

Joel gestured at the house. "After you, Harper."

Harper waved goodbye to Maisie and Trish, then dug the key out of the manila envelope and let them inside.

Joel squinted in the darkened foyer of the modular log cabin–style house. A hallway bisected the kitchen-diner and living room, where the furniture was covered with dust-thick sheets. Beyond it were two bedrooms and an upstairs loft. Dust caked the credenza table in the small entrance, and the still, hot air smelled stale.

Harper didn't say a word as she passed him, moving into the kitchen. Her gaze swept over the room's decades-old appliances, chipped-linoleum countertop and two outlets that must have overheated at some point, because the once-white plastic was now black-brown and singed.

She knitted her brow. "This is not what I wanted."

At least she wasn't lying about it anymore. Joel's gut burned, though. She hadn't ever wanted to know Clark, or else she would have contacted him before an inheritance was involved. And even though Clark had never seen a photo of her, much less met her, he'd given her a massive gift. Yet she wasn't thankful?

He couldn't hold his tongue any longer. "It's what you were given, but no one said you have to keep it. There are several good Realtors in town. Elena Santos, for one. Call her and she'll sell it for you. You can go back to Phoenix. To-morrow, even."

"That's not what I meant. I told you already I came here to meet Clark. To get answers about what happened before I was born. All of *this* never entered my mind." She touched the red rickrack trim of the dingy-white kitchen curtain, tracing the curvy S pattern with her forefinger. The graze of her finger on the vintage fabric was gentle. Reverent, almost. "I've never lived in a house before. The thought of owning one? I can't process it."

Diffused afternoon light from the kitchen window illumined her features, giving her skin a rosy glow. She was lovely, Clark's granddaughter. She might be a hundred other things, including a liar, but it was undeniable that she was beautiful, and there was no artifice in her appearance. She wore her hair in a simple style, her makeup was understated and her pale green knit dress complemented her coloring.

But he wouldn't be swayed by her appearance. Nor could he trust her or her innocent claims of wanting answers, not part of Clark's estate.

Why was she still lying about everything?

Joel wouldn't fully rest until he figured out what Harper was up to.

Chapter Three

Squawk!

The peacock's cry startled Harper again, but this time, she didn't jump into Joel's arms. She cringed inside. Why, oh why, had she done that? Ugh.

She was already self-conscious, raw from all she'd learned so far today. Of all the things she thought might happen, spending the afternoon with a cranky lawyer who was built like an action-movie star was not on the list.

Nor was coming into possession of a house.

She dropped her hand from the hand-sewn kitchen curtain. "Do you know why my mother left Widow's Peak Creek? Did Clark confide in you?"

"Not about that, no."

Plenty of other things, though, from the sound of it. Enough to make Joel judge Harper and her mom so harshly that he clearly didn't believe Harper's story about not receiving his letters.

Well, Joel might not be a lot of help when it came to learning Clark's side of what transpired between him and her mom thirty years ago, but she'd ask God to provide help from another source.

Like Trish. Her new neighbor with a passion for genealogy could point her in a good direction for research or maybe even share stories about her mom. The town wasn't so large that they would never have met, if Trish had lived here all her life. She'd have to stop by her store and invite her out to dinner.

Not tonight, though. The events of the day, including her long drive here, were catching up to her. She needed a hot shower and a solid night's rest.

"I think I'll call it a day." She left the kitchen, and Joel's footsteps sounded behind her.

To her surprise, Maisie and Trish had come back to the house and were seated on the porch steps, beside the trail of ants.

"We're back." Trish clutched the banister and hoisted herself up to standing. "Maisie has a question."

Joel's hand cupped Maisie's narrow shoulder. "What's up, Bug?"

"Not for you, Daddy. For her." Maisie's brown eyes fixed on Harper.

An energizing burst of curiosity shot through Harper's veins. "What can I help you with?"

The little girl squinted. "How do you do your hair like that?"

"This?" Harper patted her messy bun. "Easiest thing in the world. Want me to do yours? You've already got an elastic in your hair, and that's all we need."

Maisie's eyes widened. "Yes."

"Yes, *please*," Joel nudged.

Was it Harper's imagination, or was he watching closely? What, did he think she was going to hurt Maisie? He might think she was dissatisfied with inheriting an olive grove, but that didn't mean she was a monster.

Guiding Maisie so she faced away from Harper, she slipped her finger and thumb beneath the elastic, which she stretched and twisted. Then she wove the ponytail through again, stopping just before she reached the ends of Maisie's hair. She fluffed out the loop so it fell in a cute bun-shape with tendrils escaping from the bottom. "All done. Easy-peasy."

"Daddy can't do it," Maisie said.

"I should be able to now that I've seen someone do it." Joel rubbed the five-o'clock shadow on his chin. "I was cinching it in a big loop, and it didn't look right."

Ah, so that was why he'd watched her so closely.

He needed a tutorial in girl hair. "Soon you'll be able to do it yourself, Maisie."

"But until then, thanks." Joel offered a nod.

"Happy to." He may be a grouch, but since she became a Christian a year and a half ago, she'd made a point of trying to be helpful. Even to grouches.

Besides, Maisie seemed like a cool kid. There was something about the little girl that tugged at Harper's heartstrings. Maybe it was that her mom had passed away or that her left eye didn't quite seem to match the right. Or maybe it was that she reminded Harper a little of herself when she was a kid. Skinny limbs, freckled, with a reddish-blond cowlick sprouting right over her forehead.

Trish seemed nice, too, and Joel… Well, he had positive traits. Like the love he had for his little girl. And being held in those strong arms for the briefest of moments had made her feel safe.

Okay, it had felt more than safe. It had felt *nice*, to be honest.

But that didn't change anything. He thought the worst of her, believing she knew about Clark and his inheritance. It wasn't worth convincing him otherwise, but the whole thing still stuck in her craw.

Good thing their business was complete. It

was easy to smile when she bid him goodbye. It always felt good to be done with unpleasant things.

"Harper! Nice to see you." On Monday afternoon, Trish waved from the far side of a large oak worktable near the back wall of her gourmet-food store, The Olive Tree. She looked harried but happy, surrounded by kids wearing bright-colored aprons.

Harper had come to invite Trish for a coffee or out to dinner sometime, but she'd clearly interrupted a kids' cooking class. Judging by the delectable aroma of basil and bread, they were making pizzas.

"Thanks, Trish. What a lovely store." Harper could wait for Trish and the kids to finish, and in the meantime, she would enjoy perusing the store's wood shelves.

Jars of pickled vegetables sat alongside olives, nuts, crackers and sausages, inspiring thoughts of a picnic lunch or charcuterie board. A refrigerated section held cheeses, fruits and smoked fish, and in the corner behind the worktable where the kids had their class, she could see a sink and oven.

Her mother would love this place—not just the foods and the historic brick-and-wood construction of the 1850s-era building but also the way Trish incorporated a kitchen area for lessons. Harper added The Olive Tree to her mental list of things to share with her mom when they could finally talk. Not that the store was as important as the other things they needed to talk about, like Clark's passing.

Pain twinged in Harper's midsection. How would her mother respond to the news about Clark's death? Harper had grown up under the impression her mom had been orphaned, because she never mentioned her own parents, other than the fact her mother had died a long time ago and after that, she didn't have a family anymore. In fact, Harper had always thought her mom grew up in Arizona until she found that letter mentioning her home in Widow's Peak Creek, California.

Why had her mother kept silent about the past? Harper's first assumption was that Clark had been cruel. That didn't match Joel's effusive opinion of him, or Trish considering him "dear," but some people were good at putting on a persona that hid their true selves.

She would never know Clark for herself, but she knew her mother. Sheila Price was hardworking, independent and honest—about everything except her past, it turned out.

Harper had certainly given her mom ample opportunity to set the record straight about where she came from. Harper hadn't exactly asked questions about her grandparents, but she'd asked a million of them about her father. Her mom's short response that they simply didn't know each other well was never satisfying. She craved more knowledge.

What was his name? Did he know about her?

Not even expressing interest in knowing her father's health history persuaded her mom to divulge his name, though. Instead, she insisted Harper was better off letting sleeping dogs lie.

As if discovering one's parentage was akin to disturbing a hound from a nap.

"Hi, Harper."

The small voice tugged her from her reverie, and she turned toward the table of kids using child-safe plastic knives to slice pepperoni, tomato and other toppings. Maisie, in a blue-striped T-shirt, waved.

"Hey, Maisie." Harper exchanged a smile with Trish, which she interpreted as an invitation to approach the table and speak further to Maisie. "Making pizza?"

"Yes, but the basil won't cut right." Maisie's attempts with the fragrant herb had resulted in ragged chunks and green smears on her olive wood cutting board. Two taller girls across the table giggled, and Maisie's cheeks pinked.

Trish was helping another child slice a slippery olive, so Harper leaned closer to speak in Maisie's ear. "I've got a trick. Roll up that basil leaf so it looks like a tube, and then, and starting at the tip, slice it into thin pieces. Like the stripes on your shirt."

Maisie's eyes narrowed in a skeptical look, but she followed Harper's directions. Then her mouth formed an O. "They're skinny and curly."

"Called slivers. They're not the same as the chopped look you were going for, but they're pretty. And when I do it, it looks better than when I chop."

The girls across the table copied the rolling trick. Maisie grinned at Harper.

The bell over the store's door chimed. "Well, this is a surprise."

Harper recognized that grumpy voice.

Joel crossed the store toward them. He looked nice in navy dress pants and a white button-down with a subtly striped tie around his neck. He was handsome every which way, except for his glower and declaration of *surprise*, which clearly had to do with her being here. Was he upset to see her in general or because she'd helped Maisie with the basil?

Her jaw clenched hard enough to hurt her molars. His sour attitude toward her was based on the lie that she'd known Clark had existed and had chosen to disregard him until he died and left her an olive grove. Nothing she could do or say would make him believe her, so why bother trying?

She took a step back, holding her hands up in a gesture of apology to Trish. "Sorry for intruding on the class."

"No, I was glad you came over." Trish stepped around the dark-haired boy she'd been helping. "That was a great tip you showed Maisie, but I'm sure you didn't come here to slice basil. Is there something I can help you with in the store?"

"I hoped to invite you out to coffee or dinner, that's all."

"I'd love that. How about dinner tonight?"

"It works for me." If all went well, she could get some genealogy tips and start work on her family history tomorrow.

"Can you make it at five, when I close? These French bread pizzas have given me a hankering for the real thing, and DeLuca's is just down the street. Best pizza in town."

"Perfect. See you there." In the meantime, Harper could easily lose herself in the other interesting stores on the street, like the antiques shop and bookstore.

"Joel, you and Maisie come, too." Trish's grin was almost excited at the prospect.

Harper's stomach lurched. She'd far prefer to

speak to Trish alone. Joel already knew about Clark, but she didn't want to include him in further conversation on the topic. Nor could she speak freely in front of Maisie.

Joel didn't look thrilled, either, but with Maisie jumping up and down at the idea, he grudgingly agreed, as if he, too, could tolerate another hour in Harper's presence.

One hour of pizza and awkward small talk. They'd survive. Maybe while they were eating, she could set up another time to talk alone with Trish.

And perhaps she could squeeze another micron of information about Clark from Joel before the evening was through.

A few hours later, Joel choked on his bite of DeLuca's special and washed it down with a gulp of root beer. What was Trish thinking, offering Harper a job?

"Are you okay, Daddy?" Maisie scooched closer to him on the red vinyl bench they shared in the pizza parlor booth, patting his back.

"Peachy." It came out a little rough, but at least he'd stopped choking. "Wrong pipe."

So far, the evening's conversation had been light as the foursome dug into a large combination pizza and a family-sized garden salad with Italian dressing. As usual, the food was delicious—the pizza crust, crispy on the outside and soft and bready inside; the salad, fresh. But now, Joel wasn't sure he could eat another bite.

Harper…working for Trish at The Olive Tree? Staying around town and getting cozy with his family? His neck and shoulders tensed up.

Trish peered at Harper, seated beside her across the booth from Joel and Maisie. "I don't know how long you plan to be in town, but the kids' cooking classes only last a few more weeks. My employee who was running them, Goldie, had to leave town over the weekend when her daughter had her baby a month early. You're a natural, so I thought I'd ask if you'd be interested."

Joel wanted Harper gone from town, not growing roots. Even shallow ones. "You probably have a job to get back to, though. Right, Harper?"

"Actually, I'm currently unemployed. The restaurant where I worked closed down a week ago. A short-term gig sounds great while I figure things out. Thanks."

Figure out what? She made it sound like a job thing, but it didn't make sense if she was just here to get her inheritance and run with it. It wasn't like she was going to work as a pastry chef—or whatever she'd said she was—here in Widow's Peak Creek.

Meanwhile, Maisie's eyes were as round as the slices of pepperoni on her pizza. "Does that mean you'll be my cooking teacher?"

"I guess so." Harper grinned. "I already have a lot of ideas."

Trish sipped her root beer. "Just tell me what you need in the way of ingredients, and I'll ensure we have them on hand."

"Wonderful." Harper looked genuinely excited.

The familiarity of her smile struck Joel in a nice way, but he had to shove the pleasant feeling away. She may have Clark's smile, but that didn't mean she was the same type of amazing person he was.

Sure, she was nice to Maisie. The two of them talked about making chocolate-dipped strawberry ladybugs, much to Maisie's rapture. But just because she was nice to his kid didn't mean Harper wasn't a greedy liar.

He'd have to keep an eye on her a while longer if she was staying in town until the children's cooking classes ended. Why *was* she staying in town? She'd said she wanted to know more about Clark, but Joel didn't believe her. It made no sense, unless she was telling the truth about not knowing her grandfather had existed.

He was still pondering the matter when they left DeLuca's, separating to their cars. Harper's, an older model that looked as if it were held together by prayer alone, was parked closest. While she waved goodbye and clambered in, Trish mussed Maisie's hair. "I'm happy to take Maisie part of the day tomorrow if you need it."

"That would be great." She'd been a huge help, and just as horrified as he'd been about Kjersti scheming to marry Joel and get her hands on Maisie's rumored inheritance. "Hopefully, we'll find another nanny soon."

Joel wasn't sure he wanted another nanny after Kjersti, but he didn't have a choice. He couldn't rely on friends and family to help with Maisie every day for the foreseeable future, so he'd contacted the agency he'd used in the past. So far, he hadn't had a single nibble on the position.

Trish eyed him askance. "And the *other* issue?"

He appreciated Trish's use of code to refer to Joel's other problem—that of Maisie's biological father contesting Joel's attempt to adopt her. He'd fired back a strong response to the man's legal team, but no one had replied. "Nothing yet."

A clicking noise from Harper's car drew him around. She sat behind the wheel, eyes narrowed in frustration, as her car failed to start. It sounded like the battery was dead.

And even if she were lying to him through her teeth, he couldn't just leave her here.

He met Trish's concerned gaze. "Do you mind if I stay to lend a hand?"

"I'd be disappointed if you didn't. I'll take Maisie to your place so we can visit Fluff. Come when you're able." Trish gathered Maisie and they strolled off, hand in hand.

Harper stepped out of her car. "I don't suppose the local mechanic is still open?"

"I'm sure the shop is closed for the day. Sounds like it's probably your battery, though. I'd be happy to give you a jump. If that doesn't work, I can give you a ride. Where are you staying?"

Her answer made his stomach sink. That motel didn't have the safest reputation. "There are lots of B and Bs in town, if you want something different."

"I just lost my job, remember?" Her smile was self-deprecating. "Money is tight."

"It wouldn't be if you sold the grove." What was stopping her? If she was after Clark's money and nothing else, it made sense to talk to a Realtor.

"I'm not ready to sell it. Or leave town. I want more information."

About what? Much as he wanted to probe the topic, he should take advantage of the empty parking space beside hers before someone came along to claim it. "Hang tight while I go get my truck."

In his absence, she'd propped up her car hood, and thankfully, the parking space beside hers was still free. He pulled into the spot and shut off the engine. After retrieving the extra-long cables from his emergency roadside kit, he carried them to the front of his car. "What information are you talking about? The value of the grove?"

Her eyebrows met in the middle as she gave him a look of befuddlement. "No, about Clark. I told you, I want to know what happened between him and my mom. It's obvious you don't believe me, but I want to know why you and everyone else thinks he's so amazing when my mom said we had no family."

"I think your mom is the only one who can tell you why she lied." He looked up from connecting the red cable to the positive terminal of his car battery.

"Maybe it's not a lie. Maybe Clark is the one who severed ties."

"Then why did he send her letters?"

"That's what I'm trying to figure out. This is my fourth day in Widow's Peak Creek, and I'd hoped to have a lot of answers by now. But I was down with a migraine all weekend, and today's sleuthing hasn't turned up much."

"You've been *sleuthing*?" The word sounded like it was straight from a black-and-white detective movie.

"At the public library." With an exasperated huff, she took the end of the red cable and connected it to her battery. "Skimming old newspaper articles that mentioned my family, hoping to learn something. Unfortunately, I didn't get much from the accounts of my mom's high school tennis matches or Clark's service groups' pancake-breakfast fundraisers. I gave up on the newspapers and shifted to my mom's school yearbooks to see who she might've dated. Not that a photo of a guy's arm over her shoulders would have been definitive, but it would've given me something to work with. A name to start with."

Maybe Joel was paying more attention to unwinding the black cable than to her words, but what he'd heard didn't make sense. The pancake fundraisers were legendary in Clark's social life, but the rest? "You've lost me. Why were you looking at your mom's yearbooks?"

"Because… I came to Widow's Peak Creek to do more than meet my grandfather and learn why my mom never spoke of her past."

Vindication flooded his veins, hot and triumphant. "I knew you were hiding something from me."

"I'm not here for the inheritance. Everything

I told you was true." She met his gaze squarely. "But I didn't tell you I'm searching for my father. I want to know who he is."

The cable slipped between his fingers. "What?"

She picked it up for him. "I hoped my grandfather could tell me."

"You don't have any idea who your father is?"

"My birth certificate is blank under 'Father,' and my mom refuses to discuss the topic. It's eaten me up inside. For years. That's why I was searching that memorabilia box in the first place. She left for her bucket-list trip, and I took advantage of her absence by snooping. It paid off when that letter I discovered led me here. Of course I would have liked to meet my grandfather, but at the same time, my feelings about him are complicated by his relationship with my mom." Her eyes were tearless but drowning in agony all the same. "This is such a mess. All I wanted was to know who I am."

Joel let out a long, slow breath.

That look in her eyes? He'd seen it a hundred times in the mirror after Adriana died. Reflecting his pain. His uncertainty. His need for God's strength to carry on. That look couldn't be faked. Not even by award-winning actors.

She was telling the truth, wasn't she?

Not that he disbelieved Clark. Never. But this

wasn't a fabrication. Sheila Price had lied to Harper her whole life. Angry as he was at Clark's daughter, a wave of pity washed over him for Harper. "I'm sorry I didn't believe you. And I'm sorry you're struggling. That's gotta be tough."

"I don't want you to think I had a bad childhood or anything. My mom is great. It's just in this particular aspect, we're at complete loggerheads."

"Your mom lied to you, Harper—"

"Don't disparage my mom. You don't know her."

"You're right. All I know is she returned Clark's letters for years, and she's on some pleasure cruise rather than here with you, answering your questions."

"You make it sound malicious of her, but that's not it at all. She's a chef, and she's on a culinary cruise that she's saved money for my entire adult life. She has never done anything like this for herself—ever. She's sacrificed everything for me. The restaurant where she works is transitioning to a different type of cuisine. Like me, she's at a crossroads in her career, and she was hoping the classes she's taking on this cruise would spark something for her, give her direction."

"Still, she didn't tell you her father was alive."

"I know she must have had her reasons for

keeping the truth from me." She took the black cable from him.

"If you say so." He held up his hands.

She didn't attach the cable, though. She froze to the sidewalk. "Joel?"

"Need a hand?"

"No, I—what sort of lawyer are you?"

"Family law."

She flapped her hand like that was not what she'd meant. "I mean, how do you do business? Some lawyers find every loophole they can to win a case. Their methods might be legal, but that doesn't mean they're just or right."

Was she insinuating he was a snake in the courtroom? "I'm not that sort of lawyer. I learned from the most ethical man of them all. Your grandfather."

"Okay, then if truth matters to you, help me uncover it. Old newspaper articles and yearbooks aren't cutting it. I need documents, something to help me find out who my father is. Since you're a family lawyer, this sort of thing is in your wheelhouse, right?"

Not exactly, but her desperate gaze implored him and, at the same time, soothed him with the comforting familiarity he saw there. She was Clark's flesh and blood. He owed his mentor everything.

And—he couldn't believe he'd changed his mind on this—none of this was Harper's fault.

"All right. I'll help you."

"Thank you, Joel." She hopped up on her tiptoes to hug him.

His chin tipped back as the crown of her head brushed his throat. It had been so long since he'd hugged anyone other than Maisie, other than a side hug with Trish or someone from church. What happened with Harper the other day due to the peacock didn't count. This embrace was as surprising as that had been—and as awkward, maybe, too.

But that didn't mean it wasn't…pleasant.

About the time he started to hug her back, she slipped away. He turned to fuss with the black cable, glad for an excuse not to look at her. *Your nerves are shot, that's all.* Joel took a deep breath. His life had been in a tailspin lately.

She clamped the cable onto her battery. "Can you start on it tomorrow?"

She looked so happy, he hated to burst her bubble. But she should be prepared. "Yes, but I'm going to need something from you in return."

Chapter Four

ᴄ◅

An ominous chill slithered down Harper's back. Joel would help her, but only if he received something in return? Her brain scrambled, at last settling on something that made her stomach sink. "How much is your, um, hourly charge?"

She should've thought of that earlier, and she probably couldn't afford his legal services.

"I don't want payment." Joel stared down into her face, his tone soft. "What I need is your assurance that you'll be okay with whatever you learn about your father. Have you considered Sheila won't discuss it because she's protecting you from something?"

She appreciated his gentleness regarding a difficult topic, but he needn't have worried. "That's one of the only things she ever told me. She wasn't hurt by my father. Not physically, anyway. But emotionally, she was deeply wounded. I've caught flickers of grief on her face when I've asked about my dad. He broke her heart. I've pieced together that between his rejection and Clark's lack of support, she felt she had no recourse but to run away."

His expression didn't lighten. "There could be something else she wants to shield you from. Your father might not be a nice guy, Harper."

He was trying to be kind, but she'd had her whole life to think about this. "I think it's more likely that my dad was a self-absorbed kid who was too scared to stand by my mom. You're a family lawyer, so you deal with adoption, right? Most parents just want to give their babies the best lives possible. To my mom, that meant life without my dad. I'm not after a relationship with him or anything, but I would like to know who he is."

"Okay, then," he said in a way that made her think he wasn't totally on board but wouldn't back out. "But you need to know—unless there was something filed in the legal system between him and your mom, I'm limited in what I can uncover. But I will try." He handed her his cell phone. "Give me your number, and I'll text you so you have mine. Later on, let me know the name of the hospital where you were born, that sort of thing. The fastest way to find the truth, though, is your mom."

As if she hadn't tried. "Her lips are sealed tighter than a bad clam's."

Joel checked the clamps on the jumper cables. "Have you thought of doing a DNA test?"

"Doesn't it just give you a list of countries your ancestors came from?" Mom always said their forebears had been English. While she'd seen advertisements for DNA kits, she'd never wanted to spend money on something that would only tell her what she already knew.

"When Trish did it, it not only provided that sort of information but also gave her a list of genetic matches to explore."

Excitement zipped through Harper. "They could provide names of people I'm related to?"

"Only if they've taken the DNA test on that site and given permission to being contacted. I forgot to mention that part, so you shouldn't get your hopes up—but you never know. She's connected with several cousins through the website." He gave her the name of the company Trish had used. "Some of the cousins chat online occasionally."

Harper wasn't so naive that she expected to learn her father's name off the bat. It would be too much to hope that he had taken the test and consented to being contacted. But could it be possible that one of his relatives—*her* relatives—was on the site?

"If there's even one person on there that I'm related to through my dad, it would be amazing. They wouldn't even have to talk to me. I mean, I hope they would, but just having a name could give me a place to start researching. I'll look into it tonight."

"As long as you're prepared to accept the outcome, whatever it is."

"I appreciate your concern, truly, but I'm okay." More than okay. Super excited. "I think it's important to know the truth about where we came from. Or at least have the choice to know. Don't you?"

It was clearly the wrong thing to ask. Joel's face hardened, his jaw clenching so hard a muscle twitched in his cheek. "Not always, no. Some people don't understand what a privilege it is to be a parent. Children are better off without those types of people in their lives."

She'd struck a nerve. "I can't speak to anyone else's situation. Just mine. I can handle it."

"Well, Maisie can't," he blurted.

What did Maisie have to do with this? "I wouldn't tell her about this. That would be incredibly inappropriate."

Laughter carried down the sidewalk. Harper turned to see a family approaching. The woman held hands with a boy and a girl, her black knit dress hanging loosely over a softly rounded tummy that gave away the fact she was in her second trimester of pregnancy. The dark-haired man with her saw Harper and Joel first, and his lips stretched into a grin. "Hey, Joel, is it pizza night for you, too?"

"I'm stuffed." Joel rubbed his flat belly, but his smile didn't reach his eyes. "Harper Price, meet the Santos family. Tom, Faith, Logan and Nora. Guys, Harper is our new neighbor. She joined us for dinner, and I stayed back to help her with her car."

Harper heard him loud and clear. He didn't want his friends to think there was anything romantic going on between them. Fine. She wasn't in town for romance, and if she were, she wouldn't be looking at Joel Morgan.

But his words stung a little anyway.

"Price?" Tom's eyes widened. "Are you related to Clark?"

She braced herself. "I am."

"Sorry for your loss. Clark was such a kind, generous guy."

So everyone said.

Faith was eyeing Harper's car. "Too bad you're having car problems. I'm glad Joel was around to help out. He has tools for everything."

"Well, he is a contractor." Tom's eyes took a teasing glint.

What? "I'm confused. You're a lawyer." Although she had wondered why a lawyer had such a large storage box in his truck bed. It must be full of tools.

Tom laughed. "Lawyer, contractor, rugby legend."

Ah, she'd been right when she thought he looked like a rugby player. "Legend? What does that mean?"

Joel rolled his eyes. "Tom's exaggerating, and it was a long time ago."

Tom scoffed. "You're being modest. If it hadn't been for that back injury, you could've gone on a few more years."

He shrugged, as if eager to change the subject. "The important thing is I can still give Maisie piggyback rides."

"Where is Maisie, anyway?" The little girl, Nora, fisted her hands on her hips.

"She's home with her aunt Trish," Joel said. "I'll tell her hi for you, though."

"By the way, I'm sorry about Kjersti leaving town. Such a shock." Faith's voice took the low, sad tone often used at funerals or after breakups. "I'm here if you need anything."

Who was Kjersti, and why would Joel be upset by her leaving? Curiosity burned in Harper's chest, but it was none of her business if Joel had a lady friend. Or had just parted ways with one.

"Thanks." Joel took a half step back from his friends, signaling his desire to talk about something else. "We should let you get to your pizza."

Logan, the little boy, popped to attention. "I've been waiting all day for pizza."

Everyone laughed, but Harper didn't miss the curious look Tom gave Joel. Then he turned a friendly gaze to Harper. "Nice to meet you."

"You too." Harper followed Joel's lead and returned to the cars. "Are you ready to give this a try?"

"I am." He tinkered with a clamp. "But what I said before about Maisie, when we were talking about fathers? I didn't mean to imply that I feared you'd tell her about your circumstances. It's something else that makes the topic a little sensitive for me. I'm not Maisie's biological father."

"I figured that out when she mentioned something about being a Morgan soon. I take it you're adopting her."

"I'm trying to, but Sebastian—he's her father. He's decided to contest the adoption. Not only that but he now wants custody. Ironic, considering he's been out of the picture since before

Maisie was born. He abandoned Adriana—my late wife." His eyes darkened. "He didn't even show up the day Maisie was born. It was one of the worst days of Adriana's life."

"Because Sebastian abandoned her? I can see how that would be rough." And sad. Her own mom had always said Harper's birthday was the best day of her life.

"Not quite. Adriana was relieved he wasn't there. She was six months pregnant when she learned Sebastian wasn't with her for the right reasons."

Whatever that meant.

"Naturally, she broke up with him. To cheer her up one day, her parents took her out for lunch. They were divorced but trying to be there for her, a united front. Anyway, the car was hit head-on. Adriana's mom died at the scene. Her father, Doug, sustained brain damage, impeding his ability to walk and speak. And Adriana went into labor a few months early."

Wow, he hadn't been kidding about it being a horrible day for Adriana. "How awful. I don't know how a person handles that much tragedy all at once."

"Adriana was strong. She pushed through it and helped her dad through his struggles, which now include cardiac troubles. Maisie inherited her mother's fighting spirit, and it has helped her with the challenges she's faced along the way. You may have noticed her amblyopia."

Harper didn't know the word, but when Joel gestured toward his left eye, she nodded. "It doesn't always track."

"She wore an eyepatch for years. Got bullied for it, too, and she's still teased about wearing glasses—not that she talks to me about it. When she was younger, I could go to the other kids' parents, but now that she's a little older, she doesn't want me getting involved." He rubbed the back of his neck. "I know kids are kids, but it kills me when she's hurt like that. Is it wrong that I want to protect her?"

"Of course not." Harper's heart ached. "You're right, though. She's growing up, and she needs tools to handle situations so she'll be able to care for herself when she's an adult. But you being protective? That's a good quality in a dad."

And in a friend. She looked away, thinking of how grumpy he'd been with her when they'd first met. Now she knew he'd behaved that way because he cared about her grandpa and feared she was lying to get her hands on Clark's material goods.

Joel didn't respond, as if he were so lost in thought he couldn't hear her. "I might not be able to be with her minute by minute to protect her from all the bullies of this world, but when it comes to Sebastian and his sudden interest in getting full custody? I'll do all in my power to keep her safe. Sebastian isn't worthy of her. He just wants…trouble." Joel shut his eyes for a moment.

"If he hasn't been around, that proves he doesn't have her best interests at heart."

"If he did, the last thing he'd do is put her through a custody fight where she's the flag in a game of tug-of-war."

For a half a second, she thought he intended to say something else, but when he turned away, she didn't probe. She'd learned there was a difference between someone wanting to inform another and someone wanting to talk *through* something with another. This was definitely the former.

Too bad he didn't want to talk through it, because she had a few thoughts on the matter. If Maisie didn't know her biological father, she'd have questions later, just like Harper did. She could press the point with Joel, but she didn't know the whole story or what was best for Maisie. Every situation was different. "It sounds complicated."

"Let's focus on something a lot less complicated." Joel pulled out his keys. "Give me a minute after I start my engine before you start yours."

"Got it."

But as she sat behind the wheel of her car, her thoughts were on their conversation, not her battery. She'd come to Widow's Peak Creek to get answers. Unlike little Maisie, Harper had long ago dealt with the fact that her father probably hadn't wanted her. It had hurt, yes. But she'd moved past it.

Then again, maybe she hadn't, since that wound had driven her here.

Joel waved from his car, indicating she should attempt to start her engine. It sputtered to life. *Phew.* Joel gave her a thumbs-up.

Who was this guy, anyway? A dad. Lawyer. Contractor. Rugby "legend," whatever that meant. But how had he ended up in Widow's Peak Creek?

Maybe he'd needed something here, the same as she had. Not answers, perhaps, but a new start.

She'd suffered her share of hurts. It was a good reminder that everyone, even someone who gave as bad a first impression as Joel, bore pain from his or her past, too.

Thursday morning, Joel's head ached so much it felt like it would split open. Anger did that to him. Anger and fear—an emotion he was not accustomed to experiencing.

Yesterday, he'd taken a call from Sebastian's attorney, requesting a meeting. Joel had eagerly agreed, offering his office space for their discussion this morning. Surely he could make Sebastian and his counsel, Lawrence Applebaum, see sense. It was not in Maisie's best interest to be yanked from his care.

But Sebastian hadn't even shown up this morning. Lawrence Applebaum, with his fuzzy brown eyebrows and smug demeanor, had come loaded for bear, as Clark would have said. Eager for confrontation and certain Joel would roll over.

Joel had no intention of giving in, and he shoved aside the paperwork Sebastian's attorney had brought. "There's no way Sebastian will be awarded custody, and you know it, Mr. Applebaum."

"Larry, please."

Joel wasn't fooled by the attorney's oh-so-casual approach. It was a ploy to make Joel feel more comfortable and let down his guard.

It wouldn't work, not with Maisie's well-being on the line. "Judges don't look favorably on parental abandonment, as you well know. *Larry.*"

"Sebastian never abandoned Adriana or

Maisie." Larry's bushy brows rose. "Adriana denied him access."

Flames of indignation lapped Joel's skin. "That's a lie."

"Do you have proof?"

"Of his abandonment? Maisie's never met Sebastian or spoken to him on the phone. I can attest to that. So can she." Not that he wanted her to. The point of all this was to keep Maisie out of the courtroom, protected from trauma.

"If he's never met her or spoken to her, it's because you made it impossible for him to do so."

Joel's mirthless laugh was sharp in his throat. "Want to hire a tech expert to go through my phone and see if I've received and erased any messages from him? Get a warrant and go for it. It'll prove he never even tried."

"Who's to say he didn't come in person?" Larry sat forward. "Maybe you shut the door in his face, denying him access to his only child. It's his word against yours. Which is why we have no interest in mediation. It won't solve a thing. My client wants custody and we're ready to go straight to the judge."

Joel's throat tightened as he swallowed down anger.

If Sebastian and his lawyer wanted to play hardball, fine. It wasn't Joel's preferred method of resolving conflict, but it was his job to protect Maisie. No matter the cost.

"Does Sebastian still struggle with his gambling addiction?"

"We don't deny his past scrapes with illegal gambling and debt, but a more pertinent question is, are you providing an ideal environment for Maisie? No regular childcare at present. Romancing your last nanny? The abrupt end to that relationship couldn't have been good for Maisie's stability."

"What a disgusting suggestion. There was nothing between me and the nanny."

"Funny, because the topic of marriage was supposedly mentioned."

"Not by me." Who was spreading this nonsense? Nonsense that had a grain of truth to it, unfortunately. But he'd only told a few people. Like Trish and trustworthy friends.

As for Kjersti, she'd left town almost as friendless as she'd arrived. The only person he'd ever seen her interact with was Maude, an older woman at church, and they hardly knew each other.

Larry pretended to check his notes. "My client is concerned about your chaotic romantic life affecting Maisie."

"I don't have a romantic life, chaotic or otherwise."

Larry feigned surprise. "You're not seeing someone by the name of Harper Price?"

"I'm not seeing anyone, and I haven't even known Harper for a full week."

"Yet you've already been spotted embracing in public." Larry tutted.

Joel prayed for calm and looked him dead in the eye. "Harper Price gave me a brief hug to thank me for helping her—but beyond that, not a single thing you've said the last five minutes is true."

"Her mother had a reputation in this town as a troublemaker. You might want to keep an eye out, in case the trait runs in the family. Ms. Price might not be the best influence on Maisie."

Joel's fists clenched against his thighs. "Enough gossip. Let's get to the truth. We both know this is about money, plain and simple."

"Is it? Again, your word against ours." Larry capped his pen. "Look, Joel, you seem like a solid guy, so here's some free legal advice. Counteroffer for partial custody. You'd lose guardianship, but you'd still get to see Maisie on weekends and holidays—and she's what you care about, right?"

"We're done here." Joel stood. There would be no counteroffer. He was Maisie's dad, in every way that counted, and he would fight for her. No way was he agreeing to send her to live with a stranger who only wanted her money.

He was still seething an hour later when he strode over to Main Street to meet Benton for lunch at Del's Café. How dare Larry try such tactics, using gossip to make a case that Joel wasn't providing the best environment for Maisie? Nothing he'd said about Joel having relationships was true, and there was nothing between him and Harper Price.

Nothing but him poking around for legal documents naming her father and an awkward hug on Main Street that had clearly been observed by someone who'd felt inclined to gossip about it.

Although he had to admit, Harper had been on his mind a lot since Monday. He'd spent over half of their acquaintance certain she was a greedy liar. He regretted that now, and he felt good about agreeing to help find her father, although he'd struck out so far.

Nevertheless, it was best that he put distance between them. He would still try to help her identify her father. Still be friendly. After all, she was working for Trish and owned the property next door, so he couldn't avoid her completely.

But he had to ensure no one perceived anything was going on between them. No more hugs or anything else that could be interpreted to mean they were dating.

And he probably shouldn't utter a word about any of this to anyone, either. He trusted Trish and his friends, but if any of them uttered a word about Joel being concerned over how his relationship with Harper was being viewed, Sebastian could twist it to his advantage. Surely his friends weren't responsible for the story about Kjersti reaching Sebastian's ear, but Joel didn't want to give his opposition any ammunition when it came to Maisie's custody.

Best to keep that part of his conversation with Larry a secret.

Chapter Five

When Joel walked into Del's for lunch, Benton was already there, sitting in a booth, studying the menu. Joel slid into the booth opposite him. "Hey. Thanks for reaching out."

"I figured since you couldn't come to Bible study yesterday, this might be a good way to catch up."

Normally, they met every Wednesday morning with a group of guys from two local churches for Bible study and breakfast right here at the café, but Joel wouldn't be able to attend their weekly meetings again until he found childcare for Maisie.

"How did your meeting with Sebastian go?"

Joel groaned. "He didn't come, but his lawyer made it clear they're going to play hardball."

"Sebastian's sudden desire for full custody is such a shock. He's never been around, and he's had months since you started proceedings to adopt Maisie. Why didn't he say anything at the start? Plus, you have the full support of Adriana's dad. Doug doesn't attend church, and he's never wanted me to call on him at the retirement village, but he used to be a pillar of this community. If he's on board with your adoption of his granddaughter, that has to count for something."

"If it comes to going to court, I think it would." Even though Doug couldn't speak well since the car accident, he'd made it clear through nodding and typing on his electronic tablet that he was in favor of Joel's adoption of Maisie. Joel was more concerned with causing Doug any stress, however, since his heart wasn't in great shape.

The server arrived to jot down their orders, and Joel took the opportunity to switch topics to something more pleasant. "Ready for your wedding? It's in, what, a week and a half?"

"Nine days until Leah and I say 'I do.' Can't come fast enough for me." Benton leaned his elbows on the table. "Leah met your new friend, by the way."

Your new friend? "Harper, you mean?"

The gossip about Joel hugging Harper must have reached Benton. Joel took a gulp from his water glass. "I wouldn't call us *friends*. I mean, she's just arrived in town. She's working for Trish. Yesterday was her first day at The Olive Tree." Last night, Trish had waxed poetic about Harper's way with both customers and food. She had also said Harper put something together for the store's sample plate with dried apricots smeared with goat cheese and topped with chopped pistachios. Sounded weird to him, but Trish had been enraptured, and apparently everyone else who'd tried it had, too, because Trish sold out of dried apricots.

Trish had said a lot about Harper last night, from where Harper had bought a new battery for her car to all her ideas for the children's cooking class. Today was Harper's first day of teaching the children's class. He wished he could be there to watch—

"Okay, you and Harper are not friends," Benton continued, dragging Joel out of his Harper-centric thoughts. "But you're the executor of Clark's estate. I wondered how you're feeling about all of it."

It? The estate? Clark's death? Or being friends-or-not-friends with Harper?

Maybe Benton was asking something deeper, making a subtle inquiry into whether or not Joel was dating again. In truth, he wasn't opposed to remarrying, but with the custody-suit mess going on, it was certainly not on his mind.

And he certainly had no intention of dating

Harper. Especially not after what had just happened with Sebastian's lawyer.

Benton's eyes narrowed. "This has to be hard on you. I mean, she's Clark's granddaughter, so I'm sure her being here has stirred up a lot of memories. That can cause a rough patch in the grieving process."

Oh, that made sense. Benton wasn't thinking of Joel's love life but his loss of Clark. Relaxing, Joel sat back in the booth. "I miss him, but I'm grateful for the blessing he was in my life. He saw something in me when a lot of other people gave up on me." Joel's mind flashed back to the end of his so-called career in sports, right before he'd met Clark. "I was about to give up on me, too."

He bit his tongue the moment the words escaped. Benton already knew about Joel's past, of course, but Joel didn't want to talk about that right now. Didn't want to even think about it, but one awful night had changed everything for Joel.

He'd failed to protect a friend.

He never wanted to be responsible for failing like that again. God had given him the ability to keep others safe physically, as well as when it came to intangible things. Like Clark's legacy. So if he'd been overzealous with Harper when she got to town, there was a reason for it.

Same thing when it came to Maisie. Not just with the custody suit, either. It gnawed at him when other kids teased Maisie for being on the small side or wearing glasses, and she deserved to feel secure.

At that moment, their server carried out their lunch plates. After grace, Joel bit into his thick sandwich of grilled chicken breast, jack cheese, roasted green chilies and Del's special sauce. Hearty, a little spicy and delicious. Benton seemed to be enjoying his avocado BLT, too, setting his sandwich down only to reach for the ketchup for his french fries.

"How's Maisie? It's got to be rough, with Kjersti leaving."

Joel had emailed Benton about Kjersti's ridiculous plan to marry him. "Maisie's okay. A little confused, but fortunately, she hadn't grown too attached to Kjersti yet. She'd only been with us a month, so that helps." Their previous nanny, a delightful older woman, had retired with her husband down south to be closer to their children.

"How's the search going for a replacement?"

"No nibbles yet on my posting through the childcare site, despite a decent wage and an amazing kid to watch. In the meantime, Shirley and Tammy at the office have been great about me working from home, and once Maisie starts school next month, I won't need much help unless I'm in court. Thankfully, Clementine could take her again today. But right now, I'm thinking no nannies for a while."

None that Sebastian and his lawyer, Larry, could accuse of being romantic partners, for sure.

"What Kjersti did must have cut to the core— hey, ladies." Benton looked straight over Joel's head, his grin widening.

Joel craned his neck. Marigold Murphy, an older woman from church, stood just over his shoulder, carrying a shopping bag from The Olive Tree. Just behind her stood Harper, looking self-conscious. "Hello, fellas," Marigold said in her chirpy, high voice.

When he locked gazes with Harper, a zip of electricity shot through Joel, followed by a rush of self-scolding.

Why was he responding to her like this? Probably because Larry had suggested there was something between them. His reaction was a shock, plain and simple—just like when the peacock had scared her at the olive grove. The jolt of adrenaline coursing through his system had nothing to do with her personally.

Her smile was sure pretty, though. So was she, in an orange-flowered dress, with her hair in that messy-bun thing she'd taught him to do for Maisie—

Joel looked away, putting a stop to his thoughts.

Marigold waved away the café's hostess, who was pointing to an empty booth. "Just a minute. We want to talk to these fine gentlemen." She drew Harper square to the men's table. "Harper and I just met at The Olive Tree. You know Joel, of course, but this is Benton Hunt, our friend and pastor."

Harper grasped Benton's outstretched hand and returned his greeting. "I met your fiancée. Leah, is that right? She came into the store yesterday. Such a sweet person."

"Yes, that's her name. I think she's pretty sweet, too." Benton wore the loopy grin of a man in love. "Leah made some of those apricot things for me that you made at the store. Fantastic."

Harper brushed it off. "It's easy to be inspired by all the goodies on Trish's shelves." Then her smile slipped from eager to apologetic. "We should probably let you two eat while your food is hot."

"Speaking of which," Marigold said, "Del's is famous for their french fries. Try one of Joel's. Right off his plate. He won't mind."

Harper was welcome to a fry, but Marigold's

abrupt change of topic and bossiness needled at Joel. What was Marigold doing? Trying to switch the conversation to something lighter or force Harper to interact with Joel in a rather familiar way?

Dread pooled in his stomach. Marigold had played matchmaker to two of his friends in the past—Kellan and Liam—and they were both happily married now. Her friend at the retirement village, Rowena Hughes, had joined the matchmaking act and pushed Benton and Leah together. Was Joel now in the scope of some lovely but incorrigible matchmakers? The glint in Marigold's eyes was almost calculating.

It wouldn't work. It couldn't. Joel didn't dare fuel any gossip about him and Harper. But he was generally the sort of guy who shared his fries, and he didn't want to draw attention by being unfriendly, so he pushed his plate toward her. "She's right. You've gotta try one."

"They do look good." She selected one off to the side of the pile.

"Harper's going to be your neighbor, Joel."

"Yeah, I know she is." Sort of. She was still at the motel, not living at the grove, but he'd seen her car there a few times.

"No, I mean officially." Marigold's too-casual tone told him she thought the matter quite interesting. "She's moving to the grove."

He looked at Harper for confirmation. She couldn't answer because she was still chewing, but she nodded.

Made sense. It was far safer than the dingy motel where she was staying. "When are you moving in?"

Harper swallowed the fry. "This weekend. The water and power are being turned on tomorrow, and then I have some cleaning to do."

Much as he wanted to ensure no one got the wrong idea about them, Joel's conscience wouldn't let him off the hook. "Would it be all right if I dropped by with Maisie on Saturday morning? Those singed outlets in the kitchen concern me. I'm a licensed contractor, and I can handle that for you."

At the mention of the outlets, Harper's shoulders sagged. "Yeah, I wondered about those."

Benton dunked a fry in his ketchup. "Joel did a lot of work at the house where Leah and I will be living after the wedding. You can trust him to do the job right."

"All right. I would appreciate someone looking at it who knows what they're doing."

Benton pulled out his phone as if checking something. "Leah has a fitting for her wedding dress Saturday, so she can't make it, but I can come help clean Saturday morning."

"Me, too, with my buckets and broom," Marigold announced. "It will be a regular party." She stole two of Joel's fries.

Harper's flush deepened. "That's kind, but you all have been so nice already. There's no need to make a fuss—"

"No arguing." Marigold still had fries in her mouth.

"It's easier not to fight her." Joel shrugged at Harper, and it made him happy when she laughed.

Now that the adrenaline was wearing off, Joel had to admit that he still felt a little weird. His stomach flipped when Harper smiled at him, and his pulse was a little fast. For a guy who took exercise seriously, he wasn't accustomed to the sensation when he wasn't engaged in activity. Clearly, his meeting with Larry had affected him even more than he'd thought.

Marigold smiled when Harper nodded, and then she waggled her fingers at the booth waiting for them. "Those fries hit the spot. I'd better order some for myself. Come on, Harper. I promised not to keep you past your lunch hour."

"All right. But, Benton, may I ask what time services are on Sunday?"

"Eight and ten, and of course, you're welcome at our summer events. We've got a picnic coming up," Benton said with a smile. "Do you have a church back home?"

"Yes, my mom and I attend regularly. We both became Christians a year and a half ago."

One would think Sheila would tell the truth about Clark, then. Joel could only pray the whole mess Harper had found herself in would smooth out, for her sake.

Not that it affected him either way. He was fulfilling his duty to Clark, and helping Harper flowed from that. Sheila had clearly made some bad decisions that caused her family a lot of pain, and Harper was paying the price.

But he had his own family to worry about: Maisie.

Harper's smile might be nice, but he didn't want anyone getting any more ideas about the two of them.

Not even her.

After a filling lunch at Del's with Marigold, Harper returned to the store and tied her black staff apron around her waist.

Smiling, Trish looked up from dusting a shelf of fruit syrups. "How was lunch?"

"Fun." A little weird, too, with that whole french fry thing. People in Widow's Peak Creek must be a lot…cozier than anywhere else she'd lived. Either that or Marigold had really wanted her to taste test the fries. Joel had been a good sport about it.

* * *

As Harper straightened the inventory on the dried-fruit shelf, Trish drew alongside her with a cheeky grin. "Did you meet Marigold's new 'gentleman caller,' as she refers to him? Rex?"

"No, unfortunately, but we did run into Joel and the pastor, Benton. Marigold said he's getting married shortly."

"Romance is in the air in this town. Even for me." She adjusted her thick-framed glasses. "Can you keep a secret?"

Could she ever. "Mum's the word."

"I met someone through my genealogy club. It's early days, so I haven't told anyone else yet. Harvey lives a few towns away, but it's been lovely to enjoy his company. How about you?"

"Me?"

"Do you have a gentleman caller?"

"There was someone a while ago, but it didn't work out. His sister was one of my roommates, and things turned awkward, so I ended up moving in with my mom. It's been a little over a year now."

"Maybe you'll find someone here, then. You never know."

"I doubt it. I don't even know how long I'm staying in town." The children wouldn't arrive for the cooking class for over an hour, and the store was quiet, so Harper screwed up her courage and followed Trish behind the counter. "I wanted to ask you something. You said you're interested in genealogy."

"Oh, yes. Are you curious about your family history? The Prices have been here at least since the 1940s."

Much as she wanted to know about Clark and his family of origin, she was far more interested in learning her father's identity. "How do you do your research?"

Trish mentioned the website she used, the same one through which Harper had ordered her DNA test. To her surprise, the kit had already arrived. All it had required was a saliva sample, and then she popped it back into the mail. Hopefully, the extra money she'd paid for rush processing would yield results soon. "Where did you start, though? Does the website guide you through the research process?"

"To a degree." Trish leaned against the counter. "You can make a family tree. Start with yourself, add in the names of your parents and grandparents, and it gives you suggestions of places to look, like census data."

Grabbing a dust rag to clean while she listened, Harper pondered Trish's words. It sounded like she could learn a fair amount about her mother's side of the family, but without a name, her father's side of the family tree would remain blank.

Help me to trust You in this, Lord. Even if I never learn who my dad is.

She learned a lot from Trish as they tidied the store, even if the tips wouldn't come in handy yet or maybe even at all. Then Harper prepared for the children's cooking class. Every other thought in her brain had to wait in line—from her father's identity to her uncertainty about her future—so she was ready by the time the children arrived for class.

Once the dozen or so elementary-aged kids had donned miniature aprons and washed up, they set to work making a sweet dip to go with fruit skewers. Envisioning a rainbow of fruit on each skinny wood stick, she'd set out trays of deeply hued blackberries, blueberries, pale green honeydew, pineapple, mango chunks and bright red strawberries.

Would Joel appreciate the healthiness of the snack?

Joel? Harper's stomach flipped over. No, not just him—all the parents. Why had her brain gone to Joel and Joel alone?

Probably because she found Joel attractive. There, she admitted it. He was attractive. A little maddening, perhaps, and they weren't even friends. But there was a connection between them that she couldn't deny.

Enough of that. Such thinking wouldn't lead anywhere.

She gave an encouraging smile to Maisie as the little girl pulled a zester over a plump, ripe lemon so the fine peels fell into her bowl of vanilla yogurt. "That's right, gently over the rind. Nice work." The invigorating scent of citrus filled the air.

"Yeah, nice work, Four Eyes," someone muttered.

At least, it had sure sounded like someone said those words under his or her breath. Horrified, Harper peered at the children's faces. Each child was focused on his or her lemon. "Did someone have a question?"

"I didn't hear anything." Dalia, a brown-haired girl of eleven or so with a smug set to her mouth, shrugged.

"I didn't, either." A boy named Wynn set down his lemon and wiped his hands on the front of his apron. "I'm finished with the zest. What do we do now?"

Harper glanced at Maisie. The way the little girl focused on her lemon zest, it was hard to tell if she'd heard, and if so, was bothered.

Harper must have misheard the "four eyes" thing. Good. She shook her head as if to clear her ears.

"Next, we'll cut the lemons in half so we can

add juice to our fruit dip. Then we'll stir in honey to make it sweet. The flavors in the dip will blend while we work on the fruit skewers."

Harper instructed the children on how to halve the lemons with their plastic knives and then ream them using juicers. After that, they could measure tablespoons of honey into the dip.

"Harper?" Annie, a round-cheeked girl who looked about kindergarten age, raised her hand. "I can't stir my honey in."

It appeared most of Annie's honey coated her spoon handle and had slid over the outside of her dip bowl. What had managed to stay inside clung to the bowl. "Honey can be tricky sometimes."

"Yeah, but it's yummy all the time."

A few kids laughed at Annie's comment as Harper wiped the stem of her spoon with a damp rag. She was focused on Annie, but out of the corner of her eye, she could see Maisie reach across the table and flail her fingers. "May I have the honey, please?"

A bottle of honey was none too gently pushed toward her. "Here, small fry."

Small fry? Harper dropped Annie's spoon and stared at the girl across the table from Maisie. "What did you say, Dalia?"

Chapter Six

❧

Harper didn't enjoy confronting children, much less adults, but it seemed to be more than necessary. She wouldn't tolerate name-calling or bullying.

Dalia's blue eyes widened as if she were shocked by Harper's question. "I told her to 'try.' To reach it, you know?"

"It sure didn't sound like that." Judging by Maisie's sad expression as she stared at the dip before her, that wasn't what Maisie had heard either.

"It's what Dalia said," Dalia's friend Britt flicked her black hair over her shoulder. "She said, 'Here, you try.' It's not like Dalia can reach all the way across the table herself to give it to her."

The girls weren't using snotty tones, but their innocent demeanor seemed a little too forced.

A cold sense of unease prickled Harper's skin. Joel had said Maisie was teased by other kids for being small and wearing glasses. The other day, when Harper had helped Maisie with the basil, Dalia and Britt were the ones who giggled. At least, she thought they were.

That was the problem. She couldn't prove Dalia or Britt had said anything. She had suspicions but nothing more.

Nevertheless, she'd make her position on bullying clear.

"We're all friends here at our cooking classes. That means we treat one another with kindness and respect. If we can't honor one another with our actions and words, we're going to have a talk. And if things don't change from there, I talk to parents." Now that she'd said it, she should probably move on to lighten the mood. This was supposed to be a fun summer class, after all. "You're all doing a great job with the juicers. Logan, since you're finished with your dip, will you help me by passing out the skewers? Two per person, please."

The rest of the class went smoothly, without incident, but Harper took advantage of Maisie sticking around after class to go home with Trish. While Maisie helped her wipe down the worktable, Harper glanced up. "Did you have fun today?"

"Yeah, the dip was better than I thought it would be."

Harper laughed. "I'm glad to hear that. It was nice to see some of your friends, too."

"Nora's my best friend, but her brother, Logan, is okay too. So are Wynn and Annie, but they're younger than I am. Annie's only five."

"She's pretty small, so I appreciate how you helped her get the fruit on her skewer." Harper prayed for guidance. "Did Dalia say something to you today that hurt your feelings? Or Britt?"

Maisie shook her head.

"Because I won't tolerate talk like that. And I don't want you to put up with it, either."

"What does that mean?"

"Put up with it? I don't want you to allow anyone to say hurtful things to you."

"No one did." Maisie turned bright red, but she turned away, clearly finished with the conversation.

Harper had to let her know she wasn't alone, though. "Maybe we should talk to your dad—"

"There's nothing to talk to him about, okay?"

Harper wouldn't press, then. But she'd keep a close eye on the situation.

"Time to close the store," Trish called. "Ready, Maisie?"

"I'll take that." Harper held out her hand for Maisie's damp rag. "Want me to finish this and lock up, Trish?" It was only her second day of work, but she'd do whatever she could to help.

"I don't think there's anything here that can't wait until tomorrow." Trish jangled her keys. "Maisie and I are getting hamburgers. Want to join us?"

"Thanks, but I need to pick up some groceries. I'm moving into the house at my grandpa's grove on Saturday." It beat living at the motel. "We'll be neighbors."

Maisie squealed in delight, much to Harper's pleasure. "It'll be you, me, Auntie Trish, Daddy and Beau."

Oh, yeah. Beau. She'd forgotten about the peacock. "Does he squawk at night?"

"Not that I've ever heard, but in the daytime, I'm sorry to say he's ruined more than one nap for me." Trish opened the shop door for them. "Does this mean you're keeping the grove? Staying in town?"

"I haven't figured all that out yet, but I might as well sleep at the house while I do."

Harper didn't have an opportunity to mention the cleaning party, but that was just as well. In her experience, things like this often fell through. People meant well, but when push came to shove, they'd find something better to do.

Besides, Harper didn't want to be a burden. She was used to doing things with her mom and no one else; so if the cleaning party didn't go off as Marigold planned, that would be just fine.

Her mom hadn't received any help from anyone in Widow's Peak Creek thirty years ago. Harper wouldn't expect too much from the folks of this town, either.

Joel wasn't sure why Harper had looked so surprised Saturday morning when he and the others showed up at her new house, but her eyes widened as if she hadn't expected them to keep their word.

She was sweeping floors when he, Maisie and Trish strode into the house at the appointed hour. Benton arrived minutes later, followed by the rest of the crew. It had been fun to watch Harper's shocked expression when Tom and Faith, whom Harper had met at the pizza parlor, appeared with rakes, trowels and potted flowers to spruce up the outside, alongside Joel's friends Kellan and Paige, who settled their baby, Poppy, on a quilt to play while they hosed down the dust-caked wicker furniture on the porch.

Indoors, Marigold and two women from church, Trudie and Eileen, polished the wood furniture and cupboards with orange-scented oil, and Trish used a long-handled duster to swipe cobwebs from the corners. Liam and Clementine, newlyweds who'd cared for Maisie for him a lot this past week, wiped out the kitchen cupboards and scrubbed the sink. Meanwhile, Maisie, Clementine's niece Annie and nephew Wynn, and the Santos twins were supposedly dusting, but he hadn't seen them in a while.

The house was a beehive of activity, and the atmosphere was lighthearted. Joel whistled a tune as he finished screwing the new outlet plate into place. Better—in looks *and* utility. Joel felt assured that the wiring in Harper's kitchen was safe.

"Looks good," Liam said, nodding at the outlet.

"So does this food processor." Clementine pulled the small appliance out of a cupboard to dust it. "It's older, but it's nicer than mine at home. I had no idea this kitchen was totally stocked. Pots and pans, baking dishes, utensils, the works."

"Clark wanted a full-service place for guests, I suppose." Setting down the screwdriver, Joel smiled at his friends. "I'll be back in a few."

He wandered across the hall to the living room, where Harper was washing walls with a large sponge. The children kept her company while holding dust rags that didn't seem to be getting much use.

Harper watched Wynn and Annie with a bemused expression. "How many sheep did you say you have?"

"Lots." Annie shrugged casually. "And they're soft, but not as soft as Fluff."

"Oh, he's the softest, I've heard. Softer than a cotton ball." Harper grinned.

"I haven't seen Fluff in a long time." Nora stuck out her lower lip. "Or Kjersti. She's fun. Can I come to your house soon?"

At the mention of his ex-nanny, Joel thought it was time to change the subject, so he stepped into the room. "Wow, it looks great in here. Much, much better." The dusty sheets covering the furniture had been removed, revealing sturdy vintage pieces that weren't fashionable, perhaps, but went with the cabin-type look of the place. The coffee table and bookshelf gleamed from polishing, and it was amazing how a vacuum could make the patterned rug look red and blue instead of dingy maroon and indigo. The walls shone where Harper had scrubbed them, the color eggshell instead of blotchy beige.

Maisie scooped up her yellow dust rag, waving it in the air and sending motes flying through the room. "Look at me, Daddy. I'm Cinderella."

As dust scattered, Joel felt a sneeze coming on. He tried to hold it back, but it came out, loud and explosive. The kids burst into laughter.

"That rag looks full, Cinderella." Harper dropped her damp sponge back into her bucket of soapy water. "There are clean ones in the kitchen."

"Can we play with Poppy instead?" Maisie looked up at him with large doe-like eyes.

Hmm, which was more fun—dusting or playing with a baby? "Sure, you *may* play with her. But make sure her parents know you're with her, okay?"

"Okay," half of them yelled while running from the room.

Harper was smiling when she bent down to clean the baseboards. "They have so much energy."

"I hope they weren't bothering you."

"Are you kidding? They're fantastic. Nice kids. Which reminds me, I wanted to let you know there are a few older girls in the cooking class that I suspect are giving Maisie a hard time."

Before he could blink, his hands clenched into fists. "Who?"

Lord, I don't want anger to be my first response, but I don't know what should replace it. I'm trying to be more like You, but I've got such a long way to go.

"Dalia and Britt, but I don't have proof. I just wanted to make you aware and assure you I'm keeping an eye and ear out, okay?"

Not okay, but he had to let the situation unfold before he jumped all over it. And he needed to seek God's way to best handle it. He took a deep breath. "Okay."

"She has great friends in these kids. Now I can see the kids' parents are great, too."

"We're here for each other. A lot of them are related to each other, too. Marigold is Liam's grandmother. Eileen is Kellan's grandmother. Trudie is Paige's great-aunt."

"Paige and Kellan are the parents of baby Poppy, right?" Harper got a dreamy look on her face. "She is the cutest thing."

"Yeah." Not as cute as Maisie had been, of course.

"I can't believe they're here when they have their hands full with a baby. Same with Faith, being pregnant and all. They must all be busy with their own lives."

"No one is doing anything they aren't happy to do, Harper."

"I guess it's hard to believe anyone would be happy doing things like this for a stranger." Harper sighed. "I have to admit, I wasn't sure anyone would come."

"Why?"

"Because I've never had…help like this. It's always been me and my mom doing things. We didn't have anyone."

Maybe they could've had Clark, if Sheila hadn't been so stubborn. Her decision to leave town had kept Harper from knowing this kind of community from birth. Joel wouldn't bring that up now, though. "Speaking of your mom, is she reachable yet?"

"No. The cruise lasts another few weeks. Once she's back in civilization, though, I'll get in touch. I just don't want to tell her Clark is gone over email." Harper squeezed out her sponge. "I ordered the DNA test and paid extra for a rush. I hope I get results soon, but I'm nervous."

"I imagine. But either way, information is a powerful thing, Harper." Maybe it would give her the peace she craved. In an instant, even.

"You're right. Which reminds me, have you been able to find out anything on your end? About you-know-what?"

He stepped closer, catching a glimpse of a second sponge in the bucket. He reached into the cool water for it and started wiping down the scuffed wall. "I've looked at a few records, but nothing yet with your father's name. I know that must be a disappointment, but I'll keep looking. It's been a busy week with cases on the docket. Mainly open adoptions but also a child-custody arrangement that has the potential to get nasty. The way I look at it, the children's well-being is paramount. Sometimes the best of intentions get lost in the middle of a difficult situation. That's part of why I chose family law."

She looked up at him. "Was this before or after the rugby thing?"

"After." He didn't want to talk about it, though. Not now, not ever. "Back to your mom. Have you found any clues to help with your search?"

"No. But while no one else is around, I'd like to show you the letter I told you about. The one that started my journey to Widow's Peak Creek." She dropped her sponge into the bucket and stepped over to a leather wingback chair in the corner, which held her purse. She pulled out a business-size envelope.

He dried his hands on the cleanest-looking dust rag left behind by the kids and took the letter. As Harper had said, the envelope was blank, still waiting to be addressed after thirty years. He unfolded the yellow-edged notepaper inside. Sheila had written to "My Dear Friend," and he couldn't help wishing she'd called her friend by name.

I suppose you heard the news. I'm having a baby. Soon, in fact. I couldn't stay in Widow's Peak Creek. Just because I lied a few months ago, Daddy thinks I'm lying about the father. It will be better to raise this baby on my own, rather than in a town where everyone will look at me with the same scorn I saw in his eyes. Fortunately, I've met a few kind people who've offered me work in their restaurant. They remind

*me of you, warm and loving. Thank you for all
you did for me. I'm sorry not to thank you in
person, but I'll mail this letter as soon as I get
a stamp.*

Joel still wasn't feeling warm and fuzzy
when it came to Sheila, considering how she'd
rejected all of Clark's attempts to reconcile, but
this letter from her shifted his perspective a
fraction. There was no denying Sheila had been
wounded, and thirty years ago, she must have
been frightened, feeling alone in the world. Regardless of what had passed between her and
Clark, she had been in pain.

And one other thing: Clark hadn't believed
Sheila about the dad's identity. Clark may have
had reason not to trust Sheila, but still, this
event had fractured the family. The whole thing
was a tragedy.

"That's tough."

"I wish I knew who her 'dear friend' was.
And why he didn't believe her in something so
important."

"Much as I hate to say it, it sure doesn't sound
like Clark handled the situation well. But I can't
imagine what it was like. He was probably in
shock at the time, struggling to wrap his head
around what she was saying. It must have been
a lot to take in." He was whispering although
there was raucous laughter coming in from out-

side. From the sounds of things, the children were encouraging baby Poppy to crawl in their direction. In one of the bedrooms, the older women were singing a hymn. He doubted anyone could hear him and Harper talking.

"It's so hard to reconcile what I read in that letter with the Clark Price everyone else seemed to know. He was so beloved, but my mom was so hurt by him she had to run away. What am I supposed to do with that?"

"I don't know." But Joel was ruminating over the same thing. No one was perfect, Clark included, but he'd been pretty close in Joel's estimation. Joel had valued his numerous positive traits, his wisdom, his warmth.

Could Clark have made a mistake where Sheila was concerned all those years ago?

After all, Joel knew firsthand how easily a person could make a mistake that came with a heavy price attached.

And some things could never be made right.

Chapter Seven

Right after the church service at Good Shepherd the next morning, Harper passed the table selling tickets for an upcoming picnic and hurried out to the parking lot. Hopefully, no one would notice her running to her car.

"Harper?" a voice called from behind her.

So much for her attempt to be discreet. She turned around to greet Leah, Pastor Benton's fiancée. Her dark hair gleamed with hints of red in the summer sun. "Hi, Leah."

"You're not leaving already, are you?"

"No, I was getting something out of my car." *And trying to be sneaky about it.*

Leah looked relieved. "Do you need a hand?"

"That would be great." Harper led Leah to her vehicle and popped the trunk. She reached into a paper bag and pulled out a pastry box with a thank-you note attached. "This is for you and Benton, for your warm welcome to town. You were kind to me at The Olive Tree, and he helped yesterday when you had the dress fitting for your wedding. How did that go, by the way?"

"Fun. Which leads me to why I came after you." Balancing the pastry box, Leah dug into her purse for a pearlescent-gray envelope. "Benton and I would love if you could come to the wedding Saturday."

She was invited to their wedding? Harper took hold of the thick envelope. "I'm grateful, but—I don't know how to say this—I'm a stranger to you."

"There's no such thing in Widow's Peak Creek. Truly, we're a community here, and we'd be honored if you can join us. But it's late notice, so we understand if you're busy."

She was, sort of. She'd spent the past few evenings researching olive trees and oil production, and she'd finally heard back from the grove manager who cared for the trees. The manager had been ill, and Saturday morning was the only time he could make it over to walk through the grove with her. But Leah didn't need to know all that. "I appreciate it."

"We're just glad you're here in town." She fiddled with the pastry box. "This smells amazing, whatever it is."

"Baklava. I hope you and Benton aren't allergic to walnuts or pistachios." Carrying a large paper bag filled almost to the top with similar pastry boxes, Harper led Leah from the parking lot back toward the church patio.

"No, we're not. And I love baklava. Well, I love a lot of sugary things, to be honest." Leah pinched off a nibble as they reached the patio, then popped it into her mouth and made a happy *mmm* noise. "Where's it from?"

"My kitchen."

"You made this?"

"It's not that hard. The kitchen had everything I needed in the way of tools, and the ingredients are simple. I bought them and the pastry boxes after everyone left yesterday." Along with thank-you notes. It had felt good to be in the kitchen, though of course she missed her professional-grade tools and pans at home.

"Baklava seems pretty complicated to me."

"It's not that bad." Phyllo dough was delicate and dried quickly, but she was accustomed to working with it.

"Benton?" Leah waved over her fiancé as he ended a conversation with an older man. "Look what Harper made for us. Baklava."

Benton peered into the pastry box with an appreciative smile. "Wow, how thoughtful. When did you have time to do that, Harper?"

"I had to break in the kitchen once you all left yesterday. What better way than to make a small token of appreciation for your help?" It had given the house a homey smell, too, something familiar on her first night in a strange place. It had felt too big for her, and she'd lain awake far too long, listening to the house creaking and the yips of coyotes in the distance. But, at the same time, the house was hers, and she'd awoken refreshed and smiling.

A pair of gray-headed ladies caught her attention. "Oh, there's Trudie and Eileen. I'd like to give them their boxes, too."

Maisie ran up, blocking her. "There you are, Harper. I thought you'd left."

"Not yet. I had to get some boxes from my car to pass out."

"Do you need a helper?"

Maisie looked so eager that it was on the tip of Harper's tongue to say yes, but Joel's approach forestalled her speech. She'd sat in the back row during the church service, which gave her a full view of everyone seated ahead of her. There was no missing Joel, large and broad as he was. She'd seen him dressed up for court before, but there was something about a man dressed for church that—

Well, never mind. That train of thought was not helpful.

Clearing her throat, she met his smiling gaze. "Is it okay if Maisie helps me distribute a few boxes on the patio?"

"I wondered what was up." Joel eyed the box in her hands. "Sure, but what's in the boxes?"

"Baklava." Leah opened her box, releasing the honey-sweet smell of the pastry. "Harper made it."

Maisie stuck her nose in it. "I don't know what it is, but it smells good."

"It's a layered dessert made with thin flaky dough, nuts and honey," Harper explained. Then she handed two boxes with notes attached to Maisie. "This one's for Trudie and this one's for Eileen. I don't know their last names."

"I know who they are." Maisie took the white boxes and skipped off.

Benton excused himself to see to church matters, and Leah was signaled over by a woman on the committee to get the sanctuary ready for the wedding on Saturday, leaving Harper alone with Joel.

All of a sudden, she felt tongue-tied, which was strange because they'd talked plenty before. And about heavy, personal things. Their relationship might be hard to define, but it wasn't one founded on small talk. Now that small talk was appropriate, though, her nerves got the best of her and she couldn't think past how nice he looked.

Which was, of course, the absolute wrong thing to say to a man she wasn't interested in.

He broke the ice first, thankfully, tapping the paper bag with his enormous forefinger. "That was nice of you, making baklava despite having been on your feet for hours."

"I'm grateful for everyone's help."

"Even mine?" His teasing tone was something she hadn't heard from him before—not directed at her, anyway. "Is there any baklava for me? And Maisie, of course."

She decided to reply in the same teasing tone. "Yes, but it's mostly for Maisie."

His eyes crinkled when his smile grew. "Oh, yeah?"

"She's a good duster." Harper pretended to reconsider. "But you did repair the wall sockets in the kitchen, and you reached the high spots, washing the living room walls, so I guess you can share it evenly." She handed over his box.

"Thanks, Harper. Seriously. You didn't need to do this, though."

"I wanted to." She pulled out another box. "This one's for the Santos family, but I didn't see them this morning."

"They go to a different church—the one Leah went to before she dated Benton."

Fortunately, the baklava would keep another

day. "I'll drop it by Faith's antiques store tomorrow, then."

Maisie ran up, hands extended. "More for me to do?"

"Oh, yes, thank you." Harper passed her Trish's and Marigold's boxes. Maisie was hardly gone when an older woman with pale orange hair stepped around Joel to face her.

She shoved her wrinkled hand toward Harper. "Since no one's introducing us, I thought I'd do it myself. I'm Maude Donalson. Longtime member of Good Shepherd."

"I'm Harper Price."

"I know who you are. Clark's granddaughter, but you weren't at the memorial service. You're here now, though, all cozy with folks." Maude's grip tightened, squeezing like a blood pressure cuff, and the way she said "folks" made it clear she meant Joel. Was she implying there was something between them? She gave the impression that if there were, she wouldn't like it.

"Joel's been helpful with my grandfather's estate." Harper hoped her neutral tone satisfied Maude. Regardless, Maude was near Clark's age. Perhaps she could give her some information on her family. "Sadly, my mom and I couldn't make my grandfather's service. Did you know him or my mom, Sheila, well?"

"Everyone knew Clark. Sheila was a troublemaker—so I've heard, anyway. I wouldn't know personally. She was younger than my son, Odell, by at least ten years."

"Maude," Joel said, rubbing his forehead. "Spreading gossip never accomplishes anything good."

Harper appreciated Joel's defense, but her heart sank nonetheless. *A troublemaker.* She knew from that letter she'd found that her mom had lied about something before Harper was born. It also might explain why her mom had been so strict while Harper was growing up. Maybe her mom didn't want her to follow in her footsteps somehow.

Regardless, she had come to Widow's Peak Creek hoping for answers about her mom's past, and she had to accept them. Maude might not know much, but maybe her son, Odell, could add to Harper's understanding. "Is your son here? I'd like to meet him."

"No, he relocated for work." Maude was clearly not interested in the topic, though, the way she peered into Harper's bag. "What are you doing? If there's food involved at church, I'm the one to talk to. I run the casserole ministry that I started with Joel here's wife, and I bake the cookies for coffee time after church services. There's no need for you to provide refreshments."

"Duly noted." Harper pulled a pastry box out of the bag that didn't have a note attached. "I made baklava last night. I have far too much, though. Would you care for a box to take home and enjoy later? You'd be doing me a favor, taking some. It'll go stale before I can finish it."

"I've never been accused of wastefulness." Maude took the box. "You're welcome."

Maude was something, that was for sure. "Thanks for helping."

"Speaking of helping... Joel?" Maude ignored Harper. "Can I count on you to be at the casserole party in a few weeks? It's time to restock the church freezer."

"You know I never miss those, Maude. They were important to Adriana and they're important to me, too."

"I wasn't sure if you'd forgotten." With a curt nod, Maude stomped off.

"I'm sorry about that." Joel grimaced. "Maude wasn't at all welcoming."

Not particularly, but Harper's sense of feeling deflated wasn't due to Maude's words or actions. It had to do with the set of Maude's mouth and loneliness in her eyes. "I think I hurt her feelings. In sharing boxes with friends, I made others feel left out."

"I appreciate your attitude, but still. She wasn't kind." Joel watched Maude go with a faint smile.

"She cares about you."

"She's taken a few women who need help under her wing. Clementine, for one. Adriana was special to her, though. When Adriana first started attending church here with Maisie, before I met them, Maude helped her out. I'm not sure why she felt compelled to say what she did about your mom, though."

"My mother admitted to lying about something in her past, right there in that letter, so I'm not surprised she didn't have a sterling reputation around town."

"Maybe someday Sheila will explain it all to us. In the meantime, thanks for showing Maude kindness."

"Of course." Harper wasn't sure she'd ever be friends with Maude, but she could understand the pain of feeling left out.

Maisie ran back, this time with reinforcements, Wynn and Annie. Maisie held out her hands. "More deliveries?"

"Yes. This one's for Wynn and Annie's family." She handed them their box, smiling when they *ooh*ed. Then she gave the entire bag to Maisie. "And these are for your Sunday school teachers. There should be one more in there, too. Will you please give it to the older woman with Marigold? The one with the bedazzled cane."

The lady had a sweet smile, and Harper didn't want her to feel left out, either.

Joel was watching her with the strangest expression.

"What?"

"You seemed familiar just now. The look on your face." He appeared embarrassed to have uttered it aloud. "Makes sense. You're Clark's granddaughter."

"I saw his photo online. I didn't think I looked like him." She took after her mom, who must've taken after her own mother.

"It's more of a general sense of familiarity." He shifted his stance, as if his admission had made him uncomfortable. "Thinking of Clark gave me an idea, though. Every Sunday, Maisie and I get lunch and then visit Doug, Adriana's dad, at Creekside Retirement Village. A few of Clark's friends live there, and I often see them in the garden Sunday afternoons. I'm sure they'd be happy to tell you more about Clark. If you'd like to go at the same time, I can introduce you."

At the same time. He was making it loud and clear they wouldn't be arriving together.

It didn't matter. Chatting with these men wouldn't lead to information about her father, but she might learn a little something about her grandfather. And right now, she'd take whatever she could get.

"That would be lovely. Thank you."

"There they are." Joel pointed to the four octogenarians seated at a round table beneath a shady tree. He opened the French door and led Harper and Maisie out to the group.

"Who's your friend, Joel?" Mel, whose baldness pattern looked just like a medieval monk's tonsure, beckoned them over.

"Clark Price's granddaughter, Harper, visiting from Arizona. Harper, this is Mel, Stu, Ivan and Bert." Joel gestured to them in turn. "Mel and Ivan were both lawyers in town, colleagues of Clark's."

Bert's twinkling eyes were visible behind his thick glasses. "And Stu and I got to know him through our volunteer group. Would you care to join us? Have something to drink. We've got lemonade and iced tea." He motioned toward the two pitchers on the table and an inverted stack of squat clear glasses.

"I'd love that, thanks. In fact, I came here today hoping to meet you. I want to know more about my grandfather, and it sounds like you all knew him well."

This was the moment Joel had planned to bow out with Maisie, but she moved in to lean against Stu's chair. "Your drink doesn't look like either lemonade or iced tea."

"It's what we call an Arnold Palmer. Half of each." Stu mimed pouring two drinks into one, making the shoulder seams of his yellow button-up scrunch. "Sound good to you?"

"No." Maisie's statement was matter of fact. "I don't like tea."

"You've never had tea, Bug," Joel reminded her.

"I like lemonade, though." Maisie made herself at home, crawling into the chair beside Stu. "May I have some, please?"

This wasn't Joel's plan, but it was pretty hot out here. "One glass before we visit your grandpa." He, Maisie and Harper had driven here in two cars after eating brunch with a larger group of people, and like a lot of restaurant food, it had been salty. Truth be told, he wouldn't mind a refreshing drink. Nodding his thanks to Stu, Joel pulled out an empty chair from another table and moved it over so he was on Maisie's other side. Harper took the seat beside Ivan.

Stu offered him an Arnold Palmer. "Give Doug my regards."

"Mine, too," Ivan said before looking at Harper. "Doug Davis is the finest man in town. A generous donor to every worthwhile cause, a patron of arts and educational programs, a devoted father to Adriana. Before the accident, he was expected to be the next mayor. All that changed, of course, but it hasn't changed Doug's nature. He supports charities right and left."

"Wow, he sounds like a special man," Harper said.

Joel sipped his drink. It was the perfect beverage for a summer afternoon, and what a lovely setting to enjoy it. Pleasant company, the air smelling of grass and lavender bushes, sunlight filtering through the leaves of the tree they sat beneath and speckling their table with pops of light.

While Stu talked with Maisie about what made a perfect lemonade, Mel turned to Harper. "What would you like to know about Clark?"

"Anything. What he was like. What my mom, Sheila, was like."

"Clark was as upright as they come," Ivan said. "Hardly knew Sheila, although I do recall she had a strong will. Not a bad trait to have, of course. Makes a person stand up for what they believe in. I'm guessing you inherited that trait."

Her lips twitched. "Why's that, Ivan?"

"You're here, aren't you? Came a long way by yourself to get in touch with your roots."

Maisie perked up. "What does that mean? Touching roots?"

"*Roots* means family, where they came from, who they were." Harper smiled at Maisie. "I want to learn more about my relatives."

"I already know all of my relatives. My mommy's in heaven with her mommy and Jesus, but I see everyone else a lot. Daddy, Auntie Trish, Grandpa Doug. And in San Francisco, there's Grammy and Grampy Morgan, my aunties and uncles, and five cousins."

"What a blessing to have so many people in your family." Harper met Joel's gaze, and he was sure he knew what she was thinking: Maisie did not know all her family. She didn't know about Sebastian, her biological dad.

The sore subject gnawed at Joel, but he couldn't even bring himself to pray for Sebastian. After his meeting with Larry, Joel had started planning for a custody hearing. He'd even entertained the idea that Sebastian truly wanted to be a father to Maisie, but if so, why hadn't he asked to see her—not just in the past eight years but now that he had filed for custody? There had been no requests for a visit. Not even a photo or phone call.

If the guy was interested in Maisie only, and not her rumored inheritance, he had a funny way of showing it.

Meanwhile, Ivan had started a story about Clark's slow driving.

"At least he was quick in the kitchen, thanks

to his years of kitchen duty in the navy," Mel retorted. "Remember when he mass-produced pancakes for the fundraiser breakfast? I've never seen a man work a griddle so fast."

"Or read a recipe that fast. Put too much sugar in the batter, as I recall. No need for maple syrup."

"Maybe it was on purpose." Harper grinned. "My sweet tooth is what got me into being a pastry chef."

The conversation continued with laughter and fun stories, but Maisie didn't seem in any hurry to finish her lemonade. When she'd downed the final drops, Joel rubbed the back of her neck. "Well, Bug, Grandpa Doug is expecting us."

"I should go inside, too." Stu rose. "I'm ready for my Sunday siesta."

Ivan stretched his arms over his head. "Nothing beats a nap on the Sabbath."

Mel playfully wagged his finger at Harper. "Come see us again."

"Will do. And next time I'll bring cookies." She squeezed their hands and then turned her smile on Joel as they walked back to the lobby. "What a delightful bunch."

Joel couldn't smile, though. "I'm sorry they didn't offer the type of information you're looking for."

"Are you kidding? I learned a lot. That story about my grandpa's pancakes was hilarious."

"I want pancakes for dinner," Maisie said. "We used to do that every week."

Especially right after Adriana died. Which reminded Joel of their reason for being here. "Well, Doug's room is upstairs, so we're heading this way." The opposite of the parking lot, where her car was waiting. "See you, Harper."

"Do you think he'd mind if I come along with you?" Her tone was hesitant. "It sounds like he knew my grandpa, and I'd like to meet him."

"Sure." He led her down the hall to the elevators. "Remember, speaking is difficult for him."

"He smiles fine, though." Maisie pushed the button to summon the elevator.

"Smiles communicate better than words sometimes." Harper grinned, proving her point.

After the short elevator ride, they stepped into a short corridor. Joel paused at a half-open door and poked his head inside. "Doug? We're here, and we brought a friend."

Doug sat across the room in a comfortable armchair, his usual spot for their Sunday visits. Joel had seen numerous photos of Doug as a younger man, and he was still as handsome as he had been before the accident, if not as robust. Still, he took pains with his appearance, keeping his silver-tinged brown hair neat, wearing high-end button-down shirts and always smelling of expensive aftershave. He smiled at Maisie, returning her hug with stiff arms. Then he looked up at Harper with curiosity.

"Hello, sir. My name is Harper."

Doug offered a nod of welcome, but his brow crinkled with confusion.

"Harper is Clark Price's granddaughter. Sheila's daughter."

Doug's polite smile melted. In fact, his entire face went hard. He looked at Harper again, then looked away as if pained. Why the change?

Now that Joel thought about it, Doug's reaction to meeting Harper mirrored his own. Doug knew as well as Joel did—better, perhaps, since he'd been here at the time—that Sheila had left town and never looked back. Like Joel, he probably thought Harper had an agenda to get her hands on Clark's estate.

He'd better set Doug's mind at ease. "Harper wants to learn more about her family, so she's settling in at the little house at the grove. She took a job with Trish at The Olive Tree, too, helping with the kids' classes. Tell Grandpa about it, Maisie."

"Harper says I'm a natural in the kitchen." Maisie leaned against Doug's knee, describing various recipes they'd made. Doug's small smile was strained, and his fingers curled into fists on his lap.

Doug was clearly not comfortable, so Joel cut

their time shorter than usual. Harper offered a cheerful farewell, but her face fell when they left.

"I'm sorry," he said once they were in the parking lot. "Doug wasn't his usual self."

"Sometimes we all have off days. It's okay." Waggling her fingers in a wave, she got into her car. The starter clicked a few times before the engine sputtered to life.

It was on his lips to ask her to wait, but what was the point? He didn't have a good explanation for Doug's cold shoulder. Nor could he reach out and comfort Harper with a hug— not after their last brief and not-at-all-romantic embrace had been reported to Sebastian and twisted by Larry into something it wasn't.

The despondent look on Harper's face when she'd left Creekside Retirement Village was hard to forget, though, so three hours later, when Trish informed him she'd invited Harper to join them on a dinner picnic that evening, he didn't argue. For one thing, it was a done deal, and there was no way he could un-invite her without confiding his reasons why in Trish, and he'd prefer to keep them to himself.

For another thing, the evening might provide an opportunity for them to talk about what had happened today with Doug and hopefully move on.

The only caveat he made was that they go somewhere off the beaten track. The last thing he wanted was to be seen with Harper by whoever it was feeding information about his "chaotic romantic life" to Sebastian and his lawyer.

At the appointed time, he parked in front of her house. He and Trish got out while Maisie knocked on the door. Harper exited, and the sight of her in a flowy deep blue sundress and sandals literally made him catch his breath.

Don't go there, man. Just don't.

Trish clicked her tongue. "You look pretty, Harper, but there's been a last-minute change of plans. We're not going to Hughes Park after all. Joel wants to go to a picnic spot you have to hike to, so you might want to put on different shoes."

"It's not much of a hike," Joel said. "More of a walk, and the view is worth it. Besides, Hughes Park is always so crowded."

As he spoke, guilt needled his skin. None of those things were lies, but the main reason he'd requested they go to that spot was because being seen with her—in a way that others could interpret as a date—was a bad idea.

Was he wrong to manipulate events like this when he was doing it for Maisie's sake?

The question didn't sit well with him. After all, there was nothing going on between him and Harper. And it was expected they'd be together on occasion. They were neighbors.

"Sounds like an adventure." Her gaze dropped to assess their clothes. "And adventure doesn't come along too often. Is there time for me to change clothes as well as my shoes?"

"Absolutely," Trish said with a grin.

Joel couldn't smile, though. He felt conflicted, like he'd done everything wrong when it came to Harper. First misjudging her and now hoping no one saw them alone together.

It was for the best, though. He had to keep that at the forefront of his mind.

He just wished he wasn't remotely tempted to spend time with her. That would make keeping his distance a whole lot easier.

Chapter Eight

It didn't take more than two minutes for Harper to change into a pair of shorts, a T-shirt and tennis shoes. Would she need a sweatshirt or extra water or bug spray? She decided against bringing anything else. It wasn't like they'd be out for that long. The sun set late in the summer but not *that* late.

Trish, Joel and Maisie were lounging on her porch steps, staring at her car. Or rather, at the large blue bird making himself comfortable on the car's roof.

"Well, that's a new one for me. My car has been claimed by a peacock. Does that happen often around here?"

"He's never sat on my car that I know of." Trish bustled into the back seat with Maisie, leaving the front seat for Harper.

"He'll move on." Joel opened the car door for her.

Before she slid in, she eyed Beau, who looked quite content. "Don't scratch the paint, buddy." But if he did, who'd notice? Her car had seen far better days.

The whisper of Joel's aftershave swirled around her as she slipped into the front seat, a subtle but strong reminder of how drawn to him she felt. An inconvenient feeling, to be sure, especially since it made her self-conscious about being near him.

She should focus on something else. Anything else. "I smell fried chicken."

"It's one of Joel's specialties," Trish said as Joel exited the driveway.

The drive farther up into the foothills was breathtaking as the road gently curved between oaks and golden grasses. In less than ten minutes, Joel parked in an empty lot, where they gathered canvas bags of food from the back seat and set off on a wide gravel trail through the trees.

Maisie ran ahead and back while Trish regaled Harper with snippets of the area's history. Her breath short from the exertion of talking while walking up the slope, she pointed to the left. "That fork leads to the old Raven Mine. Nothing left there anymore, but that's where my forefathers worked."

"Maybe I'll check it out sometime." Harper

had enjoyed exploring little bits of the town, whether it was walking alongside the creek or taking lunch breaks at Hughes Park. The shady park was close to Trish's shop and was as relaxing as it was picturesque. An enormous boulder jutted into the waterway, forcing the creek into the V shape that gave the town its name. Every time she'd sat at one of the picnic tables for her lunch, she'd enjoyed the fresh air, water and people-watching, especially when children were busy on the playground equipment set up at the far end of the grass.

There would be no people-watching out here on the hiking trail, but the scenery had plenty of charms of its own. "I'll have to come back sometime and check out the ruins of the mine. Who knows, maybe there's still gold," she teased.

"I wouldn't bother. Daddy said it's all gone." Maisie sounded disappointed.

"The treasure is in the experience of us hiking and being together, Bug." Joel's mock look of anguish made Maisie laugh.

"I don't know, Daddy. I'd still like some gold," she teased back.

Joel led them off the trail, and soon the trees opened up to reveal a gorgeous vista—rolling hills ahead and a peaceful valley below, where cattle grazed on gold-green grasses dotted with trees and white and yellow wildflowers. The scene-stealers, however, were the numerous outcroppings of granite poking out of the earth like stone trees. She'd never seen anything quite like it.

Harper smiled at Maisie's enthusiastic response, which echoed her own silent one. "Your dad was right, huh? This is some view."

"I want to go climb on a rock!" Maisie practically shouted.

"Let's eat first." Joel set out foil containers of food while Harper and Trish spread a plaid blanket on the ground. Harper loaded her paper plate with fried chicken, potato salad laced with blue cheese and roasted vegetables. She took a bottle of sparkling water flavored with lime, and then Joel said grace.

"You are an excellent cook, Joel," Harper said between bites of chicken. "What a well-rounded résumé you've got. Lawyer, contractor, rugby—"

"I was a line cook in college."

"Well, thanks for including me tonight." Her smile encompassed all of them, ending on Trish, who'd been the one to extend the invitation. "I haven't done anything like this in a long time."

"If you like picnics, our church has one in August, with tri-tip barbecue and games for

the kids, followed by a praise-song singalong."
Trish forked a charred coin of zucchini.

"Sounds like a great evening." If she was still
in town, she'd go.

"I'm in a wedding on Saturday," Maisie said
around a mouthful of potato salad. "The pastor's
and Miss Leah's wedding. It's at the church."

Harper dotted her lips with her napkin. "Are
you a flower girl?"

"I'm in the choir."

"Oh, how fun. You'll get a great view of the
ceremony."

"Are you coming to the wedding?" Joel took
another piece of chicken.

Trish's eyes widened. "Benton told me they
invited you, and I know they'd love it if you
came."

Maisie beamed. "You could hear me sing."

Harper hadn't decided what to do about the
wedding because she felt like an interloper,
invited to a special event where she wouldn't
know anyone that well. Maisie's smile changed
her mind, though. "I think so. The only problem is, I have an appointment. I've been playing
phone tag with the grove manager, a guy named
Cyril. He's been ill—much better now, thankfully—but Saturday morning is the soonest he
can come by."

Trish winced. "I'm glad he's better, but that's too bad it conflicts with the wedding."

"It's early enough. I'm hoping it won't take long to go over the basics."

Joel gestured at the near-empty food containers. "What more can I serve up for you?"

"Not a thing, but it was all delicious. Thank you." Harper dropped her napkin atop her empty paper plate.

"Speaking of delicious, I'm enraptured with your baklava." Trish patted Harper's forearm. "Best I've ever had."

"I wish we had more." Maisie's tone was mournful.

Harper's heart warmed. "I'll make more soon."

"Are you interested in selling it at The Olive Tree? We can work out an arrangement. It'd be good for the store and good for getting your name out as a pastry chef."

That it would. "I'd be honored."

"We didn't bring anything as fancy as baklava, but we have cookies. Want one?" Joel got out a smaller paper bag. "I'm going to let my food settle first, but you're welcome to it."

She'd taken seconds of the potato salad, and there was no room in her stomach for anything more. "No, I'll wait, too."

"Me three." Maisie rubbed her tummy. "Unless I can go climb a rock now."

"I could stand to stretch my legs." Trish rose. "I'll go with you."

Harper chuckled as Maisie rushed off, followed by Trish. She was tempted to explore some of the granite outcroppings, too, but she needed to take advantage of this time alone with Joel. "About Doug today? I'm sorry if I did anything to upset him."

"I wanted to talk about that, too. You have nothing to be sorry about. Doug isn't normally like that. I didn't know him before his accident, but all I've ever heard others say of him is he's rich and he's charming."

"If he's anything like his sister, he must be, because Trish is a doll. But I think I know why he was upset with me being there." She'd been giving the matter a lot of thought that afternoon. "If he and my grandpa were friends, he must have a poor impression of my mother. And me, for that matter. He heard Clark's side and that was it."

"It's possible, but there's probably more to it." He looked away. "This is awkward to say, so I'm just going to blurt it out. I wonder if he interpreted my bringing you with us as something it wasn't. Like I was introducing you to him. As more than my neighbor."

"As your—he thinks I'm your..."

"Girlfriend."

"Yes. That." Harper couldn't say the word. "That's completely wrong."

"Completely."

"I've only been in town a matter of days."

"Exactly." He thumped his fist in agreement on the picnic blanket. "But I've never brought anyone to meet him before. I should've made it clear that we're not...like that."

"Nope." Even though a teeny part of her wished he didn't seem *too* emphatic about it.

"Adriana was his pride and joy. I can see where he might've felt blindsided."

Harper plucked a blade of grass while she considered her next words. She'd never know what it was like to be a father's pride and joy, would she? But that didn't mean she could begrudge another for being loved by her dad. "I guess it makes sense."

Joel stretched out his legs. "I'm sorry this is so weird to talk about."

"No, I'm glad you told me. So does this mean you never took Kjersti to see him?"

His countenance darkened, and she could've bitten her tongue right off. Why was she asking questions about his dating life as if she were jealous?

Except here—in the dusky light of a summer evening, with the occasional tone of a cowbell from below and the whisper of sage and pine in the air—she admitted to herself that she was a touch envious. She had no interest in being in a relationship with anyone in this uncertain time of her life. But despite her best intentions, it would be easy to develop feelings for Joel.

As easy as breathing.

And not just Joel. Maisie was a sweetheart. They were the perfect package, the two of them.

For someone else.

She just wished the thought didn't pinch at her.

This conversation had turned somewhere Joel never expected—from one painfully uncomfortable topic to another. "Where'd you hear about Kjersti?"

"Clementine. Benton. Faith. I don't know the context, but Benton said her leaving must have 'cut to the core,' and it's not hard to figure out you were dejected."

Phew. He'd been afraid she'd heard about Kjersti and her ludicrous marriage plot from the rumor mill. "Not dejected. I mean, the timing was terrible. But Kjersti wasn't my girlfriend. She was our nanny."

Harper stared at him for a full second before a tiny smile pulled at her lips. "Ah. That makes sense now. I just thought Clementine and Trish helping out with Maisie was a summertime arrangement."

"No, they were there for me in a pinch. Kjersti's departure was sudden." *Understatement of the year.*

"I'm happy to help if you need it."

"With Maisie?"

"Yes." She eyed him like he wasn't tracking the conversation. "Babysitting."

Joel's fried-chicken dinner petrified to stone in his stomach. In their meeting about the custody situation, Larry's suggestions about Joel dating his childcare providers had been enough for him to stop looking for a nanny altogether. He'd pulled his advertisement from the childcare site and was determined to work from home as much as possible—and when he couldn't, he relied on Trish or friends who obviously weren't romantic potential.

Especially not Harper, who Larry had already suggested was playing a role in Joel's life.

He didn't intend to stop helping her or being neighborly, even a friend; but maybe, from here on out, he shouldn't do anything that might be perceived as a date. By anyone. Especially not the busybody who'd seen their awkward hug in front of the pizza parlor.

He shifted position, moving slightly away from Harper. "Thanks, but it's covered. As for

Kjersti, the story is going around, and I'd rather you heard it from me. I fired her. Turns out she wanted to get married."

Her eyebrows pulled low. "You said she wasn't your girlfriend."

"She wasn't. I never thought of her as anything but Maisie's caregiver until I overheard her plotting to get me to marry her."

"She was in love with you?"

"Hardly." He almost laughed. "Doug was in crude oil in Southern California. Adriana's mom got half his money in the divorce. When she died, Adriana inherited her share. In the last few weeks, it's come to my attention that someone started a rumor that Adriana's money went straight to Maisie."

"Wait, you're saying that's why Kjersti worked for you? To marry you and get Adriana's money?"

"She admitted it when I confronted her. I'm convinced the rumor about the money is why Sebastian—Maisie's birth father—suddenly wants custody, too. Adriana ended their relationship when she found out he had a gambling addiction, six-figures in gambling debt and a girlfriend on the side. He was never in love with Adriana, but he sure had his eyes on Doug's money. Then Maisie was born."

"And he wanted nothing to do with Adriana or Maisie." Harper shook her head.

"No interest in Maisie at all, until whispers started about the trust Adriana set up for Maisie. She doesn't get it until she's an adult, but the gossip is that she gets a monthly stipend." Bile filled his throat. "There's no way the timing of Sebastian's newfound interest in his daughter is coincidental."

"Poor Maisie. Children should be loved, not used like that." She sipped her bubbly water. "What if you told him the rumor is false? If he learns she isn't getting a monthly stipend and all he wants is money, then he'll go away."

"That's the thing, Harper. The rumor is true."

Her jaw gaped.

"No one knows any of this but me and Doug. Well, Clark knew, and so did the women who witnessed Adriana signing the legal documents. But somehow it got out. Or someone guessed, put two and two together. Anyway, there's a trust. Maisie gets a monthly allowance in my care as her guardian. I'm not touching it, so it will be available to Maisie in the future. But when Doug passes on, all his money will go to Maisie as well."

"I can't believe someone would want custody of a child only to get her money. Or to marry you to get access to your daughter's inheritance. That's cold." Her eyes widened. "You thought I was just like them, didn't you?"

He laughed. "Can you blame me?"

"A little?" She laughed, too. "I get it, though. I showed up out of the blue looking for my grandpa. I can understand now why you thought I only wanted his money. You're protective. Not a bad thing."

Nowadays, yes. He hadn't always been that way, though. Painful memories struck him like lightning, sharp and powerful, of a past where he'd made selfish choices that had caused others pain.

God, I know You've forgiven me, but it's hard to forgive myself.

A childish squeal drew him to the here and now. Maisie plopped onto the blanket. "Daddy, I'm ready for cookies now."

"Um." His brain was still in the past, and he couldn't think straight.

"Here." Harper found the paper bag of desserts and, after giving one to Maisie, offered one to Trish, who had followed Maisie at a slower pace. "If you don't mind, I'd like to get close to one of those rocks, too. Get some pictures for my mom." She rose and pulled her phone from her pocket.

"Have fun." Joel watched her saunter down the easy slope to the closest piece of granite jutting from the earth. Harper was too easy to talk to, to confide in. To like.

But he had to keep a distance between them. He mustn't forget.

Besides, she was leaving town. Her mention of her mom reminded him anew that she was here for a purpose. She'd learn about her father, sell the grove and leave. Surely there were bigger markets for pastry chefs elsewhere.

At another time, things might have been different when it came to him and Harper. He might have allowed himself to admit how pretty she was and—nope. He wouldn't go there.

There was no use. Some things weren't meant to be.

Chapter Nine

The rest of the week was busy, and by Saturday morning, Harper was eager for her appointment with Cyril, the grove manager. He patiently answered her numerous questions, and by the time they finished up, she only had a few minutes to clean up for the wedding. She changed into a gauze floral dress, touched up her makeup and pinned her hair into a bun. She grabbed her purse and hurried out the door. But one thing was stopping her.

The peacock on her car.

"Beau, move. Please." Never let it be said she wasn't polite, even when it came to talking to peacocks.

The bird blinked at her but didn't budge. Her shooing motions didn't seem to bother him, either. Should she get closer? She didn't want to scare him, and she didn't want to find out if they scratched or pecked while wearing her best dress.

Meanwhile, time was ticking past.

"You seem mighty comfortable there, bird, but you don't belong on my car."

Not only that but he also didn't belong in Widow's Peak Creek any more than she did. Both were transplanted and, in their own ways, all alone.

Lord, what am I doing here? She needed to find out who her father was so she could get on with her life, but instead, she was…settling in. Trish had commissioned her to prepare baklava and other pastries to sell at The Olive Tree, and she'd happily complied. To their delight, the goodies were flying off the shelves.

While she loved crafting pastries, though, Harper found herself drawn outdoors, to the grove. Strange, since the kitchen was her happy place—but there was something about the trees that beckoned her. Every day, she took time to walk through the grove, often encountering Beau. She pretended he was greeting her when his head bobbed on his long neck.

The land was divided into four different groves separated by dirt paths, one grove for each for four different varieties of olive. Their names flowed from her tongue, foreign and flavorful-sounding; Taggiasca, Arbequina, Arbosana and Mission, the one variety she'd heard of. Some of the Mission olives were the oldest on the property, planted in the 1850s for the land-owner's private use.

What stories those trees could tell.

At present, the olives were a little larger than Thompson grapes but a brighter hue of green. She was afraid to touch them, unsure if they'd bruise, but she made a habit of brushing the tree bark and rubbing the leaves through her fingers like she was judging the thickness. Something about the feel of the trees was natural, pleasant down to her core.

But a sense of dissatisfaction still needled her. *How long can this last?*

Working for Trish was fun, but they'd dis-cussed several times that it was a temporary arrangement and her employee would be back within the month. Trish didn't need her to stay on past the summer, nor did she expect Harper to give up her career as a pastry chef to man the cash register.

Meanwhile, her apartment in Phoenix was sitting empty. Harper contacted her next-door neighbor, Mrs. Teegarden, every few days to check in, and she was grateful Mrs. Tee picked up the mail for her and her mom, forwarding anything important.

Then there was the waiting…for her mom to

be reachable. For the DNA test results to come back. For an answer to what she was supposed to do with her life.

While she waited, she took photos of Beau on her phone for her mom. For herself, too, so she could look back at this strange time in her life and marvel that she'd kept time with a peacock. Because surely this odd season was just that—a season.

Oh, how she yearned for God's guidance about what to do next, where to go when this season was over. All she could do was read the Bible, pray and remind herself of the verse that God's word was a lamp to her feet. He'd give her what she needed when she needed it.

She wished He'd see fit to send her peace right now.

Or maybe to at least prompt Beau to move off her car so she could go to the wedding.

It wouldn't do to be late. She hadn't been to many weddings, but she'd heard it was never a good idea to arrive after the bride had walked down the aisle. She flapped her arms at Beau, hoping he'd be inspired to move along, but as she did, she wondered if she should just stay home. She wouldn't be missed, anyway—but the truth was, she wanted to go. Benton and Leah had been sweet to invite her. And Maisie was singing. And Joel—

Her heart made a strange thump in her chest as Joel's charcoal-gray truck pulled into the driveway. What was he doing here? Didn't he and Maisie have to get to the church early for her choir practice?

He pulled to a stop and got out. *Mercy.* She'd thought he cleaned up well for church, but that was before she saw him dressed for a wedding. His dark suit should come with a warning label: "may cause heart palpitations."

His brow was furrowed as he hurried toward her. "Are you okay?"

Harper told her pattering heart to knock it off. "I was going to ask you the same thing. Shouldn't you be at church?" She peered into the truck's back seat. "Where's Maisie?"

"Already there, practicing with the choir. We were in such a hurry to get there in time, I forgot the gift. So I came home for it, and I saw you from the street, waving your arms. What's wrong? Your car?"

She went warm with embarrassment that she'd been spotted flapping her arms like a bird. "I think the car is fine, but I can't tell for sure because Beau won't move." She gestured at her vehicle.

Joel's eyes widened when he realized the peacock had chosen to lounge on her automobile. "Bad timing, Beau."

"I shooed him. I asked him nicely. He's not budging."

"You asked him nicely?" Joel's lips twitched.

"I tried honey, but I guess it's time to try vinegar." She shook a finger at the bird. "Don't you have a comfy nest somewhere?"

Joel approached the peacock head-on. "Move on, bud."

"I don't know how close to get, in case peafowl attack people."

"Good point." Joel paused. "Peacocks have spurs on their legs."

Cringing, Harper stepped back.

"I think he'd just leave, but you wouldn't want anything to happen to your pretty dress," he said before looking away. Fast.

Surely he was just being nice. "You look spiffy, yourself."

"Thanks. Maisie picked the tie."

"That explains the color." Pale pink silk.

"It matches her dress."

Ah. "She must be so excited to be singing."

"She's over the moon. But no one's more excited than the town matchmakers. Benton and Leah were pushed together by one."

"Marigold?" Harper clapped her hands in Beau's direction. He didn't blink.

"No, but she's ruthless." Joel's motions at the bird grew more aggressive.

Harper's memory flashed back to Marigold forcing her to try Joel's french fries at the café. Was that what that whole scene had been about?

Regardless, it was a strange conversation to engage in while they shooed away a peacock. For his part, Beau watched them as if he thought this was the most entertaining thing he'd ever seen.

This could go on all day, couldn't it? "You can go on, Joel. This could take a while."

"You should ride with me, then. You don't want to miss the wedding. It'll be fun, and the reception will offer an opportunity to meet people who knew your mom."

She probably imagined it, but he sounded resigned at the prospect of carpooling. She'd accept the ride, though. She was eager to go, and not just because she wanted to meet her mom's old friends. She was grateful for the people God had put in her life here, and while she had felt uneasy at first, she wanted to honor Leah and Benton today—

Before she could finish her thought, Beau shrieked and hopped to the ground in a rustle of feathers. The unexpected noise and rapid motion startled Harper enough to send her stumbling backward, adding her cry to Beau's.

Joel spun around, brows drawn low in concern. "Are you—you're laughing. I thought you were crying."

She wasn't just laughing anymore. She was full-on howling, in danger of getting hiccups, which sometimes happened when she laughed too hard. If she wasn't careful, her amused tears would wreck her mascara. She waved Joel off; but then she caught sight of Beau strutting off as if annoyed.

Joel had a nice laugh. Rich and deep. The kind of laugh a woman would want to hear every day of her life.

She brushed off the thought, taking a deep, steadying breath. "I didn't expect that. My heart is going a million miles an hour."

"Mine too." His laughter mellowed, but his smile quirked in a way she'd never seen before. "I'm not sure anyone will believe our *tail* about the peacock. They might cry *fowl*."

She half laughed, half groaned at his puns. "Tail, tale…fowl, foul. I get it. That's bad, Joel."

"I'm a dad. I tell dad jokes. Are you saying my bird puns don't *fly*?"

Already feeling silly, she laughed harder. "How many of these do you have?"

"None off the top of my head. I might have to *wing* it."

The puns were goofy, but she had a bad case

of the giggles now. "This conversation is getting *hawk-ward*."

"Speaking of awkward…" Grinning, he gestured at his truck. "We'd better get going, or we'll be late for the wedding."

True. "Thanks for the offer, but I'd better drive myself." She scooped up her cardigan sweater and clutch purse from the porch. "I'm out of baklava supplies."

"We can't have that." He was still smiling. "See you at church."

"See you. And thanks. For everything."

He waited for her to leave first—a gentlemanly thing to do, she supposed, but she felt self-conscious. Not about her driving but her feelings.

She hadn't laughed so hard in a long time. Joel wasn't just handsome and smart and a good parent. His dad jokes might be corny, but he was fun.

Squashing her attraction to him was going to be much harder than she'd thought.

Joel had been to his share of weddings, but there was something special about the celebrations he'd attended in Widow's Peak Creek. Benton and Leah's service was no exception.

The bridal couple radiated happiness, as did their families. The officiant, Leah's former pastor from another church in town, preached a message of love, not just between husband and wife but of Christ for His church.

And of course, the music was top notch, especially the children's choir. The moment Maisie joined Joel after the service, he welcomed her with a hug. "You sounded great, Bug."

"I think so, too," she agreed, fussing with her pink skirt. "I hope I'm in a wedding again someday."

"I'm sure you will be." A wave of emotion surged through Joel at the thought of her growing up and being a bride, even though the day was years off. Nevertheless, it was a good reminder of how quickly children grew, and that he should treasure every moment. "Ready to go into the reception?"

"I'm ready for cake." Rubbing her tummy in an exaggerated display of hunger, Maisie led them to the parish hall.

Once inside, Joel let out a whistle. The all-purpose room had been transformed. Miles of ivy and white-fabric bunting draped over the walls and stage, shimmering with fairy lights that also twinkled from potted trees set around the room's perimeter. White cloths, flameless candles and floral centerpieces made the church's round tables look picture-perfect.

"May I go look at the cake with Nora?" Maisie

pointed across the room to where her friend was slowly circling the cake table, admiring the tiered dessert.

"Sure." He strolled farther into the room, and at once, a thin hand grabbed hold of his arm, forestalling his movement. "Marigold?"

The older woman had taken her seat at a table among some of her friends...and Harper. As he exchanged greetings with them, he realized Harper was introducing herself to a few of the others, including Rowena Hughes, a parishioner in her nineties with coiffed silver hair and an eager expression. "We haven't met yet. I'm Harper."

"I know who you are." Rowena's voice was clear and strong. "You sent a box of baklava to me at church through some adorable couriers. It was delicious, by the way."

"I'm glad you enjoyed it."

Joel had forgotten that Harper distributed boxes to those who'd helped get the house in the olive grove ready for her, and then given leftovers to other folks who were on the patio.

Marigold offered him the last open seat at the table, but he declined with a gentle shake of the head. He should sit with Maisie, and it was just as well that he didn't hang out with Harper too much. The last thing he needed was for anyone to speculate about his love life and spread gossip that reached Sebastian. That was why it had taken him a while to offer Harper a ride when Beau was on her car. Others would see them riding together and could interpret it as a date.

His hesitation to carpool felt wrong, though. Stingy, unsympathetic. Unfriendly. He didn't want to be those things.

But he wanted custody of Maisie.

He'd be Harper's friend, but he had to be careful how they appeared to others.

Rowena clutched Harper's hand. "How is Sheila, my dear?"

"She's well, but... You knew my mother?" Harper's eyes widened.

"Oh, yes." Rowena's smile shone brighter than the beige sequins on her dress. "She did small jobs for me when she was in college. The odd bit of mending, cataloging the books in my husband's library, things like that. Then we'd have tea parties, just the two of us. She was a hard worker."

"She still works hard. She's a chef now," Harper said to Rowena. "I'm sorry, I didn't catch your name."

Joel felt remiss in not having made the introduction. "Sorry, Harper, this is Rowena Hughes."

Harper blinked. "Rowena?"

"You may have heard of me because I shoved

the bridal couple together last Christmas." Rowena laughed.

"Hughes Park is named for Rowena's family, and her nephew Marty's wife is the mayor," Marigold added.

Harper didn't take her gaze from Rowena, though. "You and my mother were close?"

"Dear friends, we called ourselves—despite the difference in our ages."

Something about that phrasing niggled the back of Joel's brain.

"My mom always said I was named for someone special. I've been keeping an ear out for another Harper since I got here—a first name or a last name. But, Mrs. Hughes, it must be you. My middle name is Rowena."

Dear friends. Joel sucked in a breath. The letter Sheila wrote thirty years ago was intended for her "dear friend." Could this be the answer to one of Harper's prayers?

Harper clutched Rowena's hand in both of hers. "A few weeks ago, I found a letter my mom wrote but never mailed—I don't know why—addressed to a *dear friend*. There was a line about her new bosses reminding her of whoever the dear friend was because they were kind. She must have intended the letter to go to you. I'll ask her when she's available."

"She's not available? That sounds rather mysterious." Rowena's silver brow arched.

"It does, doesn't it? She's on a culinary cruise through the Mediterranean, taking courses—"

"Daddy?" Maisie appeared at his elbow. "There's a kids' table, and Nora asked if I could sit with her."

"Sure." He should find a seat, too. Harper was in good hands, with a group of sweet older ladies patting her arm and asking about Sheila. This was what Harper needed, wasn't it? Why she'd come to town?

Besides, he had to reinforce that they were not here together. "Excuse me."

As soon as Maisie was situated, the bridal party entered the hall. From there, he took the last spot at a table of the single men from his Wednesday Bible study–breakfast group. It was good to catch up with them, but his gaze was drawn to Harper several times.

Every time he looked at her, she was smiling. Then after lunch, she mingled around the room on the arm of Marigold's special friend, Rex, who appeared to be introducing her to folks. She even talked to Maude and the man with her, a new parishioner named Fergus, before taking a turn holding Paige and Kellan's baby, Poppy, who was dressed for the occasion in a frothy yellow dress.

* * *

"Now it's time for the traditional throwing of the bouquet. Single ladies?" Leah held up a smaller version of her bridal bouquet. Immediately, a stampede of small feet rushed the area as little girls, including Maisie, gathered around Leah. A few stragglers came out, too—women of all ages up for a bit of fun.

But not Harper. At least, not by choice. It looked as if Marigold were dragging her by the arm toward the group. Joel could read her lips: *No, it's okay.*

Marigold was having none of it. She tugged Harper to the group and tried to leave her there, but Harper gamely called Marigold back. "You're single, too."

"Pah. I've got Rex now." Marigold beamed at her white-haired beau.

"I don't see a ring on your finger, Marigold," someone yelled good-naturedly.

"Fine." Marigold positioned herself by a stiff-looking Harper.

Maisie sidled alongside Harper, and they had a short discussion that resulted in Harper removing her pale-yellow sweater and draping it over Maisie's shoulders. Joel wasn't sure why, but the sight tugged at something deep within him.

"Ready?" Leah turned around, her back to the group. "One, two, three!"

The bouquet sailed through the air, straight toward Marigold.

Who batted it at Harper's face.

Harper's cheeks flushed red—no surprise, considering she'd been smacked straight-on by the bouquet. But the flowers were firmly in her grasp, just as Marigold had intended.

Then, to his surprise, Harper handed Maisie the bouquet. Maisie's mouth dropped open, but Harper nodded. She was giving the flowers to Maisie? For keeps?

That was sweet. She was good to his daughter and so surprisingly fun that even the episode with the peacock had brought out his silly side. He'd even let loose his bad dad jokes—

Stop right there. If he was feeling…warm toward Harper, it was due to the romance of the wedding, heightening his awareness of her.

Yeah, that had to be it.

At least, that was what he was going to keep telling himself. Because no way was he going to fall for anyone, much less Harper Price.

Chapter Ten

Once Harper put away the groceries she'd purchased at the store after the wedding, she slipped into flip-flops and stepped outside to stretch her legs.

She was weary but in a good way. The wedding had been fun, enlightening and emotional; and then she'd stayed behind to help clean up. Everyone had decided the decorations should stay up inside the church for tomorrow's Sunday service, but the parish hall had been cleared of crumbs, spills and decor so it was ready for children's chapel.

She inhaled deeply as she strolled into the trees, savoring the hints of grass and blossoms in the late-afternoon air. Some of the tension she carried in her shoulders let go, and she felt her neck and upper arms relax.

She'd been told Clark found peace walking in

the grove. Perhaps she was like him in this way. Nevertheless, she wandered to the old barn. Earlier today, Cyril told her it had possibilities— whatever that meant. She guessed he'd implied she could convert it to something…if she stayed.

She had just entered when a scraping noise drew her back out—the green gate between her property and Trish's. Joel, still in his wedding attire, had slipped through the gate, carrying a pale yellow bundle in one hand.

"My sweater," she said, drawing his attention her way. She wasn't visible from the gravel path—or anywhere else, really. One would have to be heading toward the barn to see her through the trees. "I completely forgot about it."

He strolled toward her through the trees. "Trish was concerned you'd need it for church tomorrow or something. She and Maisie are in the middle of baking cookies, so I'm the designated delivery man."

"Thanks." She took the sweater without touching his fingers and clutched it to her chest. "Did Maisie have fun at the wedding?"

"A blast. The bouquet was the icing on the cake. Thanks for giving it to her. You didn't need to do that."

"It was never mine. It was Marigold's. If the tradition holds up, I think that means she's the next bride, not me." Marriage was so far off her radar it didn't even register.

"How about you? Did you have fun? It looked like you and Rowena had a lot to talk about."

"Yes and no. She told me a few stories, but unfortunately, my mom never talked about dates. I hinted that I don't know who my father is, but she was sorry she didn't know more."

"At least you met her. She's a lot of fun."

"She told me all about the Gingerbread Gala at her old house at Christmastime. I'll have to go—if I'm here, I mean." She still had no clue what God wanted her to do when it came to finding her next job or selling the grove. "I have a house here, and the grove brings in some money—but I'm a pastry chef, not a farmer. I'm not sure about anything right now."

Especially him.

When she had first arrived in town, they had a rocky start. Things had smoothed over between them, though, and it sure felt like they were becoming friends.

Except for the spark she felt whenever he walked in a room or crossed her mind. That didn't feel like just friendship.

Cheeks heating, she tucked the cardigan she'd loaned Maisie beneath one arm. "Anyway, in a few days, my mom will disembark in Italy for her next course. I'll send her an email so it's waiting when she gets off the ship, asking her to call me. I wish I had the DNA results, but maybe once she learns I'm here, she'll tell me who my father is. And why she hid the truth from me."

"I hope you get the answers you need, sooner rather than later." He shifted his stance to lean against the barn siding. "I still think it's possible she was trying to protect you. That's why I haven't told Maisie about Sebastian. I don't want her hurt."

She mirrored his posture, leaning against the barn. "And I still think she'll have questions later. But you know best, Joel. You're a good dad."

"I pray to be. I never planned to do this alone."

"You're doing an amazing job. Everyone can see Maisie is happy and healthy. I can't imagine how hard it's been since her mother passed."

"I've had a lot of support. Trish. Clark, of course. Friends. My own family."

"Maisie mentioned your parents live in San Francisco? Not too far of a drive."

"We visit every month and FaceTime every few days. They wish we'd move there, but I don't want to uproot Maisie. They don't quite understand that."

"You're protective of her. It's your nature. You cared enough to protect my grandpa's legacy that you weren't going to allow me to take advantage of him, even though he's gone."

"I wasn't always like that. Protective, I mean."

"A big lug like you? I don't buy it."

She was teasing, but he didn't smile. "You heard I played some rugby."

"I did. And you hurt your back, right?"

"Yeah, but even before my injury, I knew a career in sports wouldn't last forever. I'd always been interested in the law, so the timing moved up. I went to school and planned to do something corporate."

"Until you met Clark?"

"Not quite. I had an internship with an exclusive law firm. Three-piece suits, company cars. It's what I thought I wanted. My family values hard work and success, and they were pleased with the future they saw for me. But I sought prosperity over serving people. It didn't end well."

He seemed uncomfortable. "You don't have to tell me about it if you don't want to."

"It's a testimony of sorts." He stared into the trees. "One night, the firm had a celebration for winning a big case. I'd buddied up with a co-worker—you know the expression 'smart as a whip'? He literally was. Set a problem to him, and *crack*, he'd have an answer for you. But he was not in good health, with chronic lung issues.

Anyway, we decided to leave the firm's party. Before we got out the door, though, some of the lawyers wanted to talk about my rugby career. It was late and my friend wanted to go home. I was yakking it up about my glory days, so my friend decided to go without me. Then he was mugged in the parking lot."

"No, how awful. Was he all right?"

"He healed up, yeah—and he forgave me for not being there. He said there was nothing to forgive, but I'm a big guy. If I'd been with him, I probably could've protected us."

"You don't know that."

"It ate me up inside, regardless. I started going to church, met God and then realized I didn't want to do corporate law anymore. I wanted to help vulnerable people. Children. Families. I got a bad reputation for leaving the firm, but Clark took me on. He mentored me in the law and in my faith, and helped me invest in this community. You see how much I owe him? Why I wanted to protect his legacy?"

"I understand now. Your ties to Widow's Peak Creek go beyond Maisie."

"But since meeting you, I've come to realize I might not be protecting her as well as I thought. I mean, I believe it's in her best interest to stay here with me, where she has doctors and friends and family. But I've also never told her about

Sebastian because I don't want her to be hurt. It was important to Adriana that we protect her as a child, but you've made me think of Maisie in the future, as an adult. I don't want her to grow up feeling she's been lied to her whole life."

She hugged the sweater again. "It's complicated, isn't it?"

"That's putting it mildly. Everything seems extra-complicated these days."

"Not everything," she said lightly. "If you're still able to make dad jokes, you can't be in too bad of shape."

He smiled at her, but then his gaze softened, shimmering in the waning afternoon light like the reflection of the moon on deep water.

Everything else faded. The olive grove, the house, the dusky late-afternoon sky. No looming DNA test results, no Clark, no Sebastian, nothing pressing on her mind. Just Joel and the curve of his well-formed lips, the breadth of his shoulders, the way he stared at her mouth. They were so close she could lift her hand and cup the side of his face—

Like she was going to kiss him? What was she doing? She pulled away, just in time to catch sight of the green gate opening again.

Perfect timing, Trish and Maisie. "Hi," she called, waving them over.

"What are you doing over there?" Maisie skipped toward them.

"Talking." Joel stepped away from Harper.

"I was going to poke around the barn," Harper added.

"It needs attention, but it has good bones." Trish had changed into black athleisure wear after the wedding, and she didn't seem to mind the dust and fragments of wood that got on her clothes when she patted the barn's siding. "Are you thinking of doing something with it?"

It all depended on whether she stayed in town, but if she did? "It's a bit large for an industrial kitchen for my pastries, but that's one idea. Then there's the prospect of converting it to a holiday rental."

"I love both of those ideas. Why don't you come over to my place for dinner tomorrow and we can brainstorm?"

"Sounds great. Thanks."

"I'll put a brisket in the Crock-Pot. There will be plenty for everyone." Her grin encompassed them all, serving as an invitation to Joel and Maisie, too.

"Yum." Maisie's eyes widened. "Can we watch a movie after?"

"Sure thing. If it's okay with your dad." Trish made a face—a half smile, half grimace—like she'd overstepped but wasn't too concerned about it. "You're free, aren't you, Joel?"

"We are." Joel's body language didn't match his tone, though. He stood stiff, his shoulders tense.

Probably because of their near-kiss. Or whatever it was… A moment. A weird moment because he'd been vulnerable with her, and surely he regretted that moment as much as she did.

Well, it wouldn't happen again. She was not in town for romance. She had other priorities, and clearly, he did, too.

After the trio disappeared through the green gate, Harper ducked back into the barn, determined to not give it another thought. *God, what would You have me do with this barn? Or should I just sell this whole place and move on? Put Widow's Peak Creek and everyone here behind me?*

She found no answers in the hot barn, void of anything but dust and signs of mice. No bursts of inspiration, no clear path ahead.

Harper would have to be patient, then. Patient and focused.

If only she could keep her thoughts off Joel for five minutes, the task might be a little easier.

Sighing, Harper returned to the house.

When she went inside, Harper changed into a comfy cotton dress and opened her laptop on the kitchen table. She owed an email to her next-door neighbor in Phoenix who was picking up her and her mom's mail. It might not hurt to draft an email to her mom, too. It would probably take time and a few revisions to get it just right. She wanted her mom to call as soon as she was free, but she didn't want to alarm her, either—

A message in her inbox caught her eye, however. The DNA company. Her results were in.

The emails she had intended to write could wait. With shaky fingers, she clicked the link.

It felt like forever, logging into the system. The first screen she saw was a pie chart of her estimated ethnic makeup. As her mom had said, her ancestors were primarily from the United Kingdom, but there were also slices in the pie representing Germany and Eastern Europe. She'd explore all the information in more depth later, but she had other details on her mind.

Heart pounding, she found the tab that said *Genetic Connections*.

At the top it said *Mother: Unknown.*
Father: Unknown.

Sighing, she sat back. It wasn't a surprise that her mom wasn't listed, since she hadn't submitted her DNA to the company. Apparently, her father hadn't, either. Nice as it would have been to have a name for him right here and now, though, she still had hope. She scrolled down, pulse racing. Maybe there would be distant cousins she could reach out to.

The next name on the website didn't list the relationship, but she recognized the name and accompanying photo avatar at once.

Patricia Davis. 1801 cM. across 44 segments. 26% shared DNA.

Trish, smiling at her from the photo of herself she'd uploaded to the site.

A hasty online search answered her questions about cM—centimorgans, a measurement used for DNA. Those who shared that amount of DNA were either grandparent/grandchild, half siblings…or aunt/niece.

Her brain jumped to a conclusion, but she needed to think methodically.

Slow down. Seek the Lord for wisdom. Take a breath.

So she did—in, out—focusing as her heart rate slowed from its frantic pace. *Thanks for being with me, God. Please help me make sense of this.*

She stepped into her sandals and rushed out to the grove to pray and walk…and reason this out. Talking to God the whole while, she marched through the trees, determined to consider all possibilities—no matter how ridiculous or unfathomable they seemed—so she could cross them off her list with confidence.

First, she had to consider the grandparent/grandchild scenario. Could Trish be Harper's grandmother?

No way. Trish was too young—maybe ten years older than Sheila.

The half-sibling thing was the next option to go over. It meant that Trish and Harper shared a parent. They obviously couldn't have shared a mother, since Sheila was younger than Trish.

Could Harper and Trish share a father?

That was a firm no, too. From what she'd heard, Trish and Doug's father had died when they were young adults, years before Harper was born. And Clark would have been too young to be Trish's dad.

The remaining option meant Trish—her friend, her boss—was Harper's aunt, the sister of Harper's mother or father.

No way were Trish and Sheila secretly sisters. The ages of their prospective parents didn't mesh for such a thing to happen.

That meant Harper's relation to Trish was not on her mother's side. It was on her father's.

Harper's father was Trish's brother, and Trish only had one sibling. She'd told Harper more than once that she had wanted more siblings when she was growing up, but she was grateful for her one brother.

Doug. The guy known by the entire town as a generous, kind soul.

What did that say about her mother, to have run away from a man like that?

As if that weren't unsettling enough, if he were her father, then Harper was Maisie's aunt. Half-sister to Adriana, Joel's beloved late wife.

Hands trembling, Harper grabbed her phone to text Joel. Then, before she tapped out a word, she dropped the phone like it was a hot brand in her palm.

She couldn't tell him this. Not now. Maybe not at all.

Her stomach churned, threatening to revolt, but she had no choice about what to do next.

It was a good thing Beau wasn't back on the roof of her car, because she had somewhere to go. Now.

Chapter Eleven

Half an hour after leaving Harper's, Joel stood at his kitchen sink, trying to figure out what to do for dinner. Or rather, that's what he should be doing, but he couldn't get his mind off what had happened back at the barn.

For a second there, it sure seemed like he and Harper had an honest-to-goodness-almost-kiss-type moment. Thirty minutes later, his heart was still thumping like he'd run to city hall and back, but it didn't make a difference. He couldn't allow himself to have feelings for her.

He scrubbed his face, wishing Trish hadn't invited them all to dinner tomorrow. Each time he was with Harper, there was the risk of being observed. He hated himself for caring about appearances, for skulking around, for hesitating to offer her a ride to the wedding, which was the sort of thing he'd usually do for anyone.

But she wasn't just anyone. Larry's suggestion that Joel had jumped into a relationship with Harper singled her out as someone he needed to be careful around.

And unlike everyone else, he was attracted to her. Drawn to her. Felt more himself when he was around her. Few people made him feel comfortable enough to share what had happened at the corporate law firm, and fewer made him feel free enough to let loose with some puns, but she'd laughed and joined in.

Harper was…different. So, he had to keep his focus on Maisie, and proceed carefully where Harper was concerned.

After the dinner at Trish's tomorrow, he should probably tell Trish he didn't want any more gatherings like that. And why. He trusted Trish, but if she slipped up and mentioned to a friend that Joel was concerned about the optics of Harper in their lives, Sebastian could twist it to his advantage.

Joel didn't want to give that man a single piece of ammunition to use against him in a custody hearing.

The loud ringtone from his phone resting on the kitchen table jolted him to the present. The name on the screen surprised him. "Maude? How are you?"

"We need to talk about the casserole party. Are you coming?"

Hello to you, too, Maude. She had a big heart but was a gruff sort of person, so he didn't take her tone personally. "Absolutely."

"Then we should discuss recipes."

"Whatever recipes you choose are fine with me. You know better than I do what freezes best."

Her sniff told him she was slightly appeased. "Is that woman coming?"

"What woman?" But he had a sinking feeling as his eyes caught on the bouquet Harper had caught at the wedding reception, sitting pretty in one of Trish's vases on the kitchen table. "If you mean Harper, she's welcome."

"You aren't joined at the hip?"

He swallowed his irritation. Maude had been close to Adriana, so maybe she was worried about him moving on.

She needn't be. "We're not dating, Maude."

Her whoosh of breath was loud over the phone. "I knew it. I said you'd never date the likes of her."

"You said? To whom?" Was it the same person who had seen him hug Harper on the sidewalk at DeLuca's and started spreading tales?

"Lots of folks. Half the people at the reception wondered if she's as much trouble as her mother was."

He rubbed his forehead. "Maude, instead of fanning gossip, you should put a stop to it. I don't know Sheila, but Harper is an honorable person. Regardless, there's nothing between the two of us. So if you hear that going around, please pour water on that fire, okay?"

They may have had a moment at the barn, but nothing like that would ever happen again.

They talked casseroles and old times with Adriana before disconnecting the call. It hadn't been a pleasant conversation, and Maude was a bit of a busybody, but her call had done two things for which Joel thanked God.

She'd given him the opportunity to set the record straight about his relationship with Harper, so hopefully, there would be no further talk of Joel's supposed dating life reaching Sebastian's ear.

Second, the conversation doused the adrenaline that had been pumping through his veins since he and Harper had had that moment.

No more of that. No more being alone with her. He didn't want anyone to get the wrong idea.

Even him.

Harper took the elevator to the third floor of Creekside Retirement Village's main building and turned down Doug's hallway. When she reached his open door, she took a moment to study him in profile as he sat reading in his comfortable chair.

Lord, please give me words. And a heart ready to receive the truth.

At her gentle knock at the threshold, he looked up with a smile that faded when he recognized her.

She screwed up her courage. "Hi, Doug. I'm Harper. We met last Sunday. May I come in for a moment?"

His mouth worked like he wanted to say no, but at last he nodded.

"I won't take up much time." She sat where she had during her previous visit. "I've heard so many good things about you, Doug. Your generosity. Kindness. I'm hoping you can help me with something."

A brow quirked like she'd piqued his interest.

"I don't know how to say this, so I'll just come right out with it. I took a DNA test, and it told me Trish, your sister, is my aunt. In the past, she's said you're her only sibling. I've gone over every other scenario there could possibly be for her and I to be related, and all I'm left with is…you. Is the DNA wrong? Should I try the test again?"

His eyes lost the brightness of curiosity, but in them, she saw other things: The gold flecks in the irises, so much like hers. The way his left eyelid dipped more than the right one, in just the same place as hers.

"No, there's no need, is there? You're my father, aren't you?"

His breath hitched.

"My mother never told me anything about you. All everyone here says is she was a troublemaker. She kept you secret from me, so maybe she kept me secret from you. Did she tell you about me? Did she rob us of thirty years together?" She placed her hand over Doug's.

To her shock, he snatched his away. "Don't..."

Don't touch him? "Okay. I'm sorry. I'm just happy to meet you after so long."

"Don't," he repeated. "Just..." He made a shooing motion with his hand.

Surely he didn't mean she should leave. Did he not understand her? "You're my father, Doug. I have DNA evidence."

Doug glared at her. Then sank to the floor.

"Help!" Harper's shout drew personnel in scrubs, and in seconds, she was rushed out to the hallway. Her prayers were half-formed, more groans than words, and she was about to call Trish when a nurse came out of the room, smiling. "He's all right now, but he needs rest."

"He's okay? Honest?"

"Honest. You can come back tomorrow to see your dad," the nurse said.

"What makes you think he's my dad?"

"Sorry, I just assumed. I'm new in town." The nurse ushered her down the hall, where none other than Marigold was setting down a large olive green Tupperware container at the nurses' station.

"Howdy, Harper. I'm just dropping off some wedding cake for the staff. Leah works in the building, you know."

"Oh, right."

"What are you doing here?"

"Visiting Doug, but he had some sort of episode. They say he'll be okay, but I'm a little shaken up."

Marigold patted her arm. "Of course you are. It was probably his heart. It's not in the best shape."

"Joel mentioned it."

"Stress isn't good for him—not that you were causing him any trouble. You were just calling on a friend of your grandfather's. Some of the folks here at CRV don't get a lot of visitors, you know. Your heart is almost as golden as Doug's is."

"He's got a sterling reputation, doesn't he?"

"Oh, yes. It's almost as if he's never made a mistake in his life."

No wonder that letter her mom had written to Rowena and never mailed said Clark didn't believe her when it came to who Harper's father was. Doug was, by all accounts, the finest man to ever walk the streets of Widow's Peak Creek.

But she was living proof he wasn't all he'd appeared to be. And his response to her declaration made her feel emptier than she'd been when she arrived in town.

She didn't have evidence, but it sure seemed like he'd known about her, all right, and kept it a secret. Maybe it was time for Harper to keep one of her own. If she told anyone Doug was her father, she'd hurt more than his reputation—she could hurt him. He'd had a cardiac episode just now because of her.

Then there was the matter of how the truth would affect Doug's family. Precious Trish. Maisie. And Joel… Doug was Joel's father-in-law.

To think, Harper had once harbored thoughts of wanting a family life like Adriana's. And then she'd gone and started developing feelings for Joel. Her half sister's husband. She'd almost kissed him earlier that afternoon.

No, no, a hundred times no.

She'd wanted answers but not like this.

She now knew who her father was. But the truth hadn't set her free. Instead, it had locked her inside a cold, lonely cage of secrets and shame.

* * *

The following evening, Harper found herself in Maisie's bedroom while the little girl waved her hand as if she were giving a tour. "This is my closet and my stuffed animal collection."

Harper had been in a downcast mood since her visit with Doug—who was doing much better, according to Trish that morning at church. Harper had called Trish about Doug's episode last night, and thankfully Trish hadn't asked what Harper was doing at the retirement village.

Trish had been so confident in Doug's well-being that she'd kept her scheduled kayak date with her new beau, Harvey, that afternoon, promising the brisket would be ready in the slow cooker for their dinner tonight.

Until they'd blown a tire. Trish then had moved dinner to Joel's house, probably without consulting him, since she'd told Harper in a group text.

Start without me. I'll be there as soon as the tire's fixed.

Harper had offered to reschedule, but Trish wanted the brisket eaten, so Harper went to Joel's at the appointed time. He had been friendly but preoccupied. Well, she was preoccupied, too. In the twenty-four hours since learning

Doug was her father, she'd experienced a gamut of emotions.

Depressed and confused as Harper was, though, it was impossible not to smile right now as Maisie showed off her toys. Maisie was adorable, precious…and her niece.

"Which one's your favorite?"

"The rabbit. His name is Fluff Two." Maisie patted the plushie atop her pillow. Just like his namesake, he was gray and soft-looking. Harper had enjoyed petting the live bunny in the long, thin sunroom a few minutes ago.

"I like your room." It reflected Maisie's personality: cheerful and sweet. Harper investigated the titles on the bookcase and admired the artwork on the wall. Then she paused by Maisie's bedside table, peering at a framed photo of Maisie as a tinier child—preschool, perhaps—wrapped in the arms of a beautiful blonde woman.

"That's my mom," Maisie said.

My half sister.

Adriana and Harper didn't look alike, which made her feel relieved somehow. But she also saw kindness in Adriana's brown eyes. Harper couldn't help suspecting they'd have been friends had they met.

"I don't remember everything anymore. Sometimes Daddy has to tell me things."

"What do you remember, then?" Harper was hungry for knowledge about the half sister she'd never know.

"She laughed more than I did when she tickled me." Maisie giggled. "She made good cinnamon toast. She did casserole parties at church, too. I don't remember those, but when we do them, it makes me think of Mommy because she started them. Are you coming to help?"

How could she say no? "Sure, but I'm not entirely sure what happens. We make up casseroles, obviously."

"In the church kitchen. Miss Maude tells a bunch of grownups how to mix up dinners to put in the freezer for sick people."

That sounded like Maude. "Do you help cook?"

"Sometimes I stir something, but mostly I run around the parish hall. Miss Maude is particular, Daddy says, and it's best if we let her do things the way she wants to. She says she's doing it Mommy's way, but I don't remember my mommy ever yelling at people over noodles."

"Are you two coming?" Joel's voice carried through the small house. "Dinner's ready."

Harper followed Maisie to the snug kitchen. She liked Joel's house—or rather, Trish's guest house. It was no more than a cottage, with two bedrooms and that narrow sunroom where Fluff the rabbit lived and Joel kept a desk. The house might be on the cozy side, but it was bright and had a happy feel to it.

Joel, dressed in a T-shirt that showed off his arm muscles, quirked a brow at Harper. "Hungry?"

The savory aroma of brisket made her mouth water. "Yes, but I feel badly digging in when Trish isn't here."

In truth, she'd been conflicted about coming at all since learning Doug was her dad. She wanted to be around Trish and Maisie, her blood relations. And, yes, Joel. He was her friend even if she had complex feelings about him.

But she had so much to process, and she was holding back the truth from them. It was to protect them, but it still felt wrong. Like a lie.

They said grace and loaded their plates with Trish's brisket, spicy coleslaw and fluffy rolls, but Trish still wasn't there by dinner's end. When Maisie suggested an animated movie for them to watch, Harper reluctantly agreed. Much as she wanted to spend time with Maisie, she couldn't shake the sense of depression gnawing at her. Nevertheless, she lowered herself onto one end of Joel's overstuffed blue couch. Maisie sat beside her, and Joel dropped on her other side, stretching one of his muscled arms over the back of the couch.

Harper snuck a peek at it. At him. Then chastised herself. What was wrong with her? This attraction to Joel was—well, it wasn't wrong *morally*, she supposed, but it was not a good thing. It was inconvenient and messy, and it had to stop. Now. Aside from the fact that she had some big decisions to make about her future, she was also keeping a secret from him, and it was a doozy.

Halfway through the movie, Trish swept into the family room, carrying a plastic bag with two cartons of ice cream in it. "Sorry, everyone. My poor tire."

"Are you okay?" Harper hopped up to help as Joel paused the movie.

Trish moved into Joel's kitchen. "Perfectly, and I'm grateful Harvey was there. I ran over a broken bottle on my way out of the parking lot. Harvey helped me with the spare and stayed with me at the tire shop. He's a gem."

"Ooh, he's your boyfriend," Maisie teased.

"Yeah, yeah," Trish teased back. "Who's up for ice cream?"

Harper dutifully sampled both flavors Trish had brought but hardly tasted them. After they finished the movie, she once again rose from the couch. "Thanks for the fun evening, everyone, but I'd better head home."

"You don't have to." Maisie pouted. "It's summer."

"And you don't have to be in the store early," Trish added.

"True, but I have a few things to do before bed." Like email her mother. She couldn't put it off any longer. She needed to talk to her as soon as her mom was off the cruise ship.

"Joel will walk you home, then." Trish waved at him.

"It's okay. It's right next door."

"Humor me," Trish said.

Harper smiled, but she knew it probably looked fake. She didn't want to be alone with Joel. Didn't want him to ask what was wrong and have no idea what to say.

Because she sure couldn't tell him the truth.

Chapter Twelve

Joel wasn't the world's most intuitive guy, but something was up with Harper. As he opened the green gate to her property, he noted the faint but present shadows beneath her eyes, like she hadn't been sleeping. And she hadn't been as chatty as usual tonight. Neither had he, to be honest, but something was definitely off with her.

"Everything okay? You look tired."

Harper didn't meet his gaze. "I didn't sleep much last night."

"Lots on your mind, I'm sure. Like finding your dad. I'm sorry I haven't found anything to help." No documents of anyone signing away parental rights, no court-ordered child support—nothing.

"It's okay. In fact, I think we should stop looking."

"Take a break, you mean? Surely you don't

want to stop altogether." It was the whole reason she'd come to town.

"I'd rather you focus on Maisie's adoption. Sebastian's push for custody. You know what I mean." She rubbed her head as if weary and distracted.

"Believe me, I am focusing on it." He didn't follow her up the porch steps. He'd been happy to walk her home—just as he'd have been happy to walk anyone home—but when it came to Harper, he had to care about appearances. "I hate it, though. I hope Maisie never realizes that all she is to her father is a payday."

"She'll find out someday, you know." Harper's voice was flat. "Maybe not everything, but she'll figure out enough. And in the meantime, secrets are heavy things to bear. Maybe you should decide if it's going to be worth it in the end. Not just to Maisie but to you."

"Are you saying I should tell Maisie her dad is a gambling addict who just wants what's in her bank account?"

Harper turned at the door. "Of course not. She's eight. But now or later, she needs to be told something, or she might be even more hurt when she's an adult." She rubbed her forehead again. "Sorry. None of my business. I just care about Maisie."

"I know you do."

Her smile wasn't convincing. "I just want you and Maisie and Trish to be happy."

Joel watched her slip inside and waited for the snick of the lock before returning home.

Wanted them to be happy? Why did that sound so cryptic? And almost like...a goodbye?

There was no future beyond friendship with Harper, so why did the thought of her leaving fill him with panic?

Sometime around midnight, Harper hit Send on her email to her mom. It was the most difficult email Harper had ever written, choosing her words carefully so her mom understood it was important they speak but it wasn't a life-or-death situation.

It *was* important, though. She had to tell her mom about Clark's passing. And Doug. It would be best done in person, but the phone was far better than an email.

She had finally settled on a simple message to her mother.

I hope the culinary cruise has been fabulous! And of course, you have two more courses to go. Tuscany and Paris! Ooh la la.

Looking forward to talking on the phone as soon as you are able.

So much to catch up on, she tacked on at the end. Thankfully, Harper didn't have to go into work until noon Monday, so she didn't set her alarm. Nevertheless, she was wide awake, praying for God's peace and guidance, when her cell phone rang at seven o'clock sharp.

"Mom?" A flutter of nerves spread through her as she sat up in bed. "I didn't expect to hear from you yet."

"I got your email, so I thought I'd give you a buzz. I only have a few minutes before my first course starts, but how are you, honey?"

"Fine." Bodily, anyway. Mentally? *Lord, help me.* "Are you already at the villa in Tuscany?"

"Yes. It's gorgeous. We're surrounded by olive trees."

Funny, so am I. "Sounds fun. But since you're on a tight timetable, maybe we can talk later—"

The shrill shriek of a peacock pierced the room.

"What was that?"

Harper sighed. "A peacock."

"You adopted a peacock and it's living in our apartment?"

Harper knew her mom was joking, but she couldn't smile. "I'm in Widow's Peak Creek."

The line crackled as the silence stretched. "I haven't heard that name spoken aloud in thirty years." Her mom's voice wavered with emotion. "How did you... What happened, Harper?"

She started with the loss of her job, then explained how she'd found the letter her mom had never mailed to her *dear friend*.

"I thought I'd mailed that. I didn't have a stamp, I remember that… Then we moved, so it must have gotten packed before I could mail it." Mom's voice wobbled. "So that's how you learned about Widow's Peak Creek?"

"I drove straight here."

It hurt to tell her Clark had passed away. "I'm sorry to blindside you with this. I wish I could've told you in person."

"No, honey." Her mom was crying now, her shock and grief painfully real. No matter what Joel thought about her mother, or what questions Harper had about her mother's past, there was no way she'd known Clark had died months ago.

After sitting with her mom in silent tears for a while, Harper told her about the inheritance, the olive grove and the DNA results coming in, which led to Trish.

And Doug.

Mom cleared her throat. "Have you met him? What did he say?"

"Not much of anything. He can't." She explained how she knew Trish and Joel, and then shared about the car accident years ago that had left Doug with verbal and mobility issues, killed his ex-wife and caused Adriana to go into early labor with Maisie. And to add to the loss, that Adriana had passed away two years ago.

"As Clark's law partner, Joel was wary of me at first, but he's since become a...friend. We dropped in on Doug. I didn't have the DNA results then, but he must've figured out who I was because he was guarded. Rude, almost. I made excuses for him, but now I think he just wanted me to go away. After I got the test results and confronted him, he had a cardiac episode. So I'll honor his unexpressed wish. I won't tell anyone he's my father."

Her mom let out a ragged sigh. "You're protecting his reputation as a model citizen?"

"For the sake of the people who love him. So I don't give him a heart attack." Their talk had taken a wrong turn. "I didn't want our conversation to go like this. I'm sorry. I just wanted to know what happened back then."

"I can't do this right now." In the background, a gong sounded. Calling the course members to meet, probably.

Harper's heart shattered. "I get it. You've got your course."

"I don't care about the course, but I need to see your face when I answer your questions. You have every right to be upset with me. If I'd told you the truth a long time ago, you wouldn't have had to go through all of this on your own."

Mom's voice was stronger now. "This can't have been easy for you."

"It hasn't." She swallowed hard. So much left to say, and yet…she couldn't say anything more at all. "Anyway, I'll email Joel's contact information to you. You only have a few weeks to claim what your dad left you."

"I'm not concerned about that at all. I'm worried about you. You're upset."

She'd never been a good actress, and she was still confused and a little angry with her mom. Angry in general. This is not at all how she'd wanted the conversation to go. "I've waited thirty years. I can wait a few more weeks until you're back from Paris."

"Harper," her mom started, only to be cut off by the gong again.

"It's okay, Mom. We'll be okay." They'd hash this out, and then they'd move forward in their lives. Harper could only pray God would show her exactly how to do it.

For the zillionth time, Joel checked his phone as he popped leftovers in the microwave for his and Maisie's lunch. Nothing from Harper. After their strained conversation last night, he'd been concerned about her; but didn't want to bug her in case she was resting. She'd seemed so tired.

But also hurt. He wanted to protect her the

way he wanted to protect Maisie, like it was an automatic setting in the software of his brain. God had made him to be a protector. A defender.

It was easier to defend on the sporting field. At least then, he could ram into his opponent and drag him down. It was physical, tangible. But how could he defend Harper from the intangible? He didn't even know what was wrong, other than she wanted to take a break from her hunt for finding her father's identity.

It was just as well that they spend less time together. He didn't want to fuel any gossip about them. The less he was with Harper, the better, right? And the less risk there'd be for falling for her.

Maisie's singing from her room was sweet, a stark contrast to his frustrated thoughts. Which reminded him yet again of what Harper had said last night. Was she right? Would Maisie need answers about Sebastian someday, too?

Of course she would. He'd been kidding himself to think it was anything but inevitable.

He didn't want to tell her Sebastian was fighting for her. Not if there was still a chance a hearing could be avoided.

But that didn't mean he couldn't introduce the topic so it wouldn't come as a complete shock later if Sebastian persisted. After all, Maisie was expecting a court date to be adopted by Joel, but it was frighteningly possible that she was about to become the rope in a game of tug-of-war between him and the biological father she'd never heard of before.

Lord, what words do I use? Adriana was supposed to decide when Maisie was old enough to know about Sebastian, but we never expected him to want legal claim over her. If she were here, she'd know what to do. But Adriana's with You, and I'm here alone.

No, not alone. He had God. And right now, he leaned heavily on Him as he left the kitchen and made his way to Maisie's bedroom.

She was sprawled on the floor, creating a floral pattern on a paper doll dress with a purple colored pencil. The sunlight hit her hair just so, making it shine like spun gold. She was growing so fast. How much longer would she make paper doll clothes? Or want posters of kittens hanging on the pale pink walls?

Memorizing the moment, he leaned in the doorjamb, folding his arms. "Hey, Bug."

"Hi, Daddy." One last flourish and she dropped the purple pencil. "Is something wrong? You have a frowny face."

He took a seat on her trundle bed. "Just wanted to touch base about the adoption."

She hopped up alongside him, reaching for her

stuffed rabbit to hug. "Do we have a date with the judge yet? Because I want to invite some people. Aunt Trish," she said, ticking off her fingers, "Grammy and Grampy, Grandpa Doug, Nora and her family because she's my best friend, and Wynn and Annie, too, and Harper."

Maisie was becoming attached to Harper. That made two of them.

"I know what I want to wear." Maisie stuck a finger in the air. "My Christmas dress."

"The green velvet one with the sparkles?"

"I want to look fancy."

"Good point. I'm going to dress up, too, but we don't have a court date with the judge yet." He cleared his throat. "In fact—"

His throat stuck. *This is so hard, Lord.* "I was wondering if you ever thought about your birth dad."

"Sometimes. I can't remember his name, though." She rested her chin atop the stuffed rabbit's head.

"Sebastian Green. Do you have any questions about him?"

"Not really."

The next question was hard to get out. "Do you ever want to meet him? It's okay if you do."

"I suppose someday." Maisie hugged her stuffed rabbit tighter. "But you're always my daddy, right?"

"That's me." He pulled her under his arm and kissed the crown of her spun-gold hair.

After a moment, she wriggled away, back to her designing. "What's for dinner?"

"I just heated up our lunch. I haven't thought about dinner."

"Yeah, but I just wanted to tell you not to make tacos."

Tacos had not been on his radar. "Sure, but why?"

"Auntie Trish told me a secret. Harper's teaching us how to make tacos in cooking class today, and I don't want to be taco'd out."

"Is that even possible? I don't think either one of us could get sick of tacos." Speaking of cooking class, though, how was she doing socially? Harper hadn't said any more about the other girls giving Maisie a hard time, but he should check in on that. "Are the cooking classes going okay?"

"Yeah."

He watched her face. "What about the other kids?"

"They're fine." Her shoulders stiffened.

"Because if there's anyone who's not nice—"

"Daddy, it's fine," she repeated.

He wanted to press it, but something inside him made him let it go. "I'm here if you need me, okay?"

"Okay." She returned to her colored pencils.

At least Harper had promised to keep watch over her during the classes. He had to trust her to help if Maisie needed it. Things might be complicated with Harper, but he knew how much she cared for his little girl.

Still, this was another reminder that he couldn't control everything. Couldn't protect the people he loved from everything bad out there. Maisie had been entrusted to him—

Entrusted. By Adriana and, he believed, the Lord. Because they'd found Joel fit for the task.

Lord, help me to give You control. He didn't like the process one bit, but he sensed God working on him. *I need You to strengthen me for the tasks that come along with raising her, including dealing with Sebastian. I want what's right for Maisie, even if it's hard for me, so help me to accept it. And in the meantime, show me what I need to do for her, Lord.*

And for Harper, too.

Caring for people was always a blessing, but that didn't mean it never hurt. Or that he'd never have to say goodbye.

And from every indication, his life was about to change in one way or another. All he could do was pray God would give him the grace to get through it.

Chapter Thirteen

Later that afternoon, Harper placed bowls of carnitas on the worktable at The Olive Tree for the children. The pork, which she'd cooked at home, smelled delicious, like peppers and spices. But with her brain still swimming from the conversation she'd had with her mom earlier, she didn't have an appetite.

"Fix up your tiny tacos however you like." She'd had the children dice avocado, shred cheese and prepare mild pico de gallo salsa. The table was a mess, but the children dove into their tacos with enthusiasm.

Almost everyone was boisterous by the time the class ended, except for Maisie. She lacked her usual cheerfulness as she helped Harper clean the worktable.

"Hey, is everything okay?" Harper watched Maisie carefully.

"I guess." Maisie looked away. "I just kind of hate my glasses."

"Do you need a new prescription?"

"No, I just hate wearing them. People think they're stupid."

Uh-oh. "Did Britt or Dalia say something about your glasses?" Harper had been watching the older girls, but she hadn't seen them say or do anything to Maisie or the other children. She'd hoped they'd taken her words about teasing and bullying to heart, but it appeared they hadn't stopped. They'd just ensured they wouldn't be caught doing it.

Lord, I need Your help with this one. I might be her aunt, but that doesn't mean I have any authority or wisdom here. All I know is I care about Maisie.

She'd never felt this way toward a child. It had started long ago, before she knew they were related by blood. And she didn't want Maisie to feel sad about anything—not if she could help it.

"I'll meet you in the break room." After a quick word with Trish, Harper paid for a box of cookies from the shelf and carried them to the small break room, where Maisie sat at the café-style table, swinging her legs. "Chocolate chip."

"Mmm." Maisie bit into one.

"I like your glasses." Harper took a cookie.

"You're the only one. You and my dad." Maisie sounded glum.

"That's not true. Aunt Trish knows a lot about stylish glasses, and she likes yours. Plus, your friends like them."

"But Dalia and Britt—" Maisie broke off. "Never mind."

"People who bully or tease others—kids and adults—are often upset about things in their lives, or because that kind of behavior has been modeled for them by the people they live with. It's kind of sad, isn't it?"

"Yeah, but it still doesn't feel good."

"That's why we should also be nice to ourselves. Just because someone lashes out like that doesn't mean we have to put up with it."

"I don't know how to stop it, though. When someone says something mean about my glasses or my eyes, I don't know what to say. I just want to run away."

"It is good to avoid bullies, for sure. But when we can't, I've found it's important to remember who you are. And you are Maisie Jane—a masterpiece."

Maisie rolled her eyes. "I'm not a 'masterpiece.'"

"Sure you are. God's children are works of art, precious and valuable. Just like paintings hanging in a museum. No way would you leave a canvas on the street so someone can drive over it. You'd protect it. We have a voice, Maisie, and when someone acts like you aren't a masterpiece, we can say no."

"You mean, stand up for yourself?"

"Yes, because you deserve to be treated well." She offered Maisie another cookie.

Trish poked her head into the break room. "Ready to go, Maisie? We're meeting your dad for dinner."

"Can Harper come?"

Panic flittered in Harper's chest. "Thanks, honey, but I have to do some baking tonight. I'll see you later, though."

"Aww." Maisie hugged her goodbye. "Are you still coming to the casserole party Saturday?"

She'd already told Maisie yes, so she nodded.

"What about the church picnic coming up? Will you come to that?"

Harper couldn't lie. "I'm not sure."

She wasn't sure about anything right now.

The whole drive home, she prayed the same thing over and over.

Lord, what am I supposed to do? Where do I go from here?

Figuratively and literally. She still had to have a big talk with her mom. Still needed real answers about what had happened thirty years ago. She trusted her mom, but all the stuff about

Doug being amazing and her mom being a troublemaker confused her. Her mom's desire to wait until they were face-to-face to enlighten her didn't help.

Sooner or later, though, she'd have to decide whether to stay in town or move on. If she stayed, what would she do for a living? Her pastries were popular, but she didn't have sales outside of The Olive Tree at this point. The grove could possibly be a moneymaker if she better knew what she was doing, but she couldn't manage it alone. Besides, her expertise was dessert, not olive oil.

Then there was the question of Joel. She fought her attraction toward him, but if she stayed, would she be in danger of falling for him? It felt like they'd known each other far longer than the actual days on the calendar page. Their friendship had gone deeper than most of her female friendships had and, in all honesty, she wasn't sure she could ever forget him even if she was struck with amnesia. She might not remember her own name, but he'd never slip from her memory.

Neither would the fact that she was his late wife's secret half sister.

The truth could cause his family distress.

It was a jumble, and all she could do was pray and wait for God's direction.

But in the meantime, she avoided him the rest of the week. When he picked up Maisie from class, she was friendly, but no more. For his part, he gave her so much space she wondered if he were avoiding her, too.

But on Saturday morning, as she parked in the church lot for the casserole party, she knew they'd have to interact. She'd have to pretend like everything was completely fine.

It wasn't. Her pulse ratcheted up when she walked in the kitchen and there he was, dispensing cups of juice to Maisie and Clementine's kids. "If you're ready for board games," he said to the children, "there are a few choices for you in the parish hall."

As the kids rushed into the adjoining room, he glanced up at her. His smile was hesitant, but oh boy, did it make her stomach flip over. As Liam joined him to talk, she turned away, trying to find her place in the room.

Alongside Trish and Joel, Marigold and her beau, Rex, had come, as had Clementine and Liam, Marigold's grandson. Also in attendance was Fergus, an older fellow clad head to toe in denim except for the yolk-yellow apron he wore that read "Have You Hugged a Farmer Today?" Clementine gave him a side hug and laughed. The group was merry, the atmosphere light.

Yet Harper's stomach ached—not from hunger but grief. She couldn't deny she was drawn to Joel. Wanted to join him in his spot by the stove and experience his teasing gaze. Just thinking about it, her fingers went to her lips.

Knock it off, Harper.

"Listen up, folks." Maude's loud voice yanked Harper from her reverie. "We're making thirty casseroles today. Ten hamburger noodle, ten apricot-chicken and rice, and ten macaroni and cheese with ham. When someone from church or the community has an illness or other need, all Pastor Benton or a volunteer has to do is take a casserole and a bag of mixed vegetables out of the freezer for them. With several pairs of hands, this should be a snap. Here's what we're going to do."

Maude gave orders like a drill sergeant, but Harper appreciated the sense of organization. Within minutes, they were all engaged in their assigned tasks—chopping onions, dicing ham or, in Harper's case, preparing the creamy sauce for the noodle casserole. From her spot at the stainless steel worktable, she had a direct view of Joel's back as he tended the stove, browning beef and sautéing thin strips of chicken.

If she looked up at him every three seconds or so while opening ten cans of condensed cream-of-mushroom soup, well, he was right there in her line of sight, wasn't he?

She wasn't the only person in the room with

a staring problem. Fergus seemed quite taken with Maude. Or at least, he was smiling like a man besotted when she pointed a gnarled finger at the cans of corn she wanted him to open for the noodle casseroles.

"Drain them first, Fergus."

"You got it, ma'am."

"Then rinse out the cans before you put them in the recycling bin."

"Absolutely, ma'am."

Maude left him to inspect Harper's handiwork. "That's right—add the condensed soups first. This is one of Adriana's recipes."

"Oh?"

"Seems fitting to include it in the rotation, seeing as these parties were all her idea." Maude's chin tilted up. "Back when she started coming to church, I took her my famous macaroni and cheese. She was in a difficult place. I suppose you heard about the accident."

Harper nodded. "I can't imagine how difficult that time must have been."

"Yet Adriana recognized the blessing a good meal could be, and she turned it around with an idea to bless others."

"That's so thoughtful." Harper wasn't surprised, though. Adriana would have to have been a wonderful person for Joel to love her. "You two were close?"

"I was her confidante. With everything. Even her financials. That's how close we were." Maude speared her with a look. "There's no replacing a woman like that. Ever."

Harper wouldn't want to try, but... Was that how Maude saw her? Like she was trying to step into Adriana's shoes when it came to Joel?

Harper's stomach lurched. She might be drawn to Joel, but she could never have been with him anyway. She'd always be the secret half sister of his beloved late wife. Second best.

Meanwhile, the woman was still waiting for an answer. Harper's mouth had gone dry, so she nodded. She hoped that was enough for Maude.

"I recycled the cans." Fergus appeared at Maude's elbow. "Shall I open the pimiento jars next?"

"Come on, let me show you." Maude sounded pleased to be needed.

"Fergus is my next-door neighbor," Clementine said in a low tone as she measured dry mustard into the apricot-sauce bowl. "We had a rough start, but he's a new man now and coming to church."

Harper could relate to having a rough start with someone. "Some relationships begin with conflict, don't they? Mine with Joel wasn't particularly smooth."

Marigold leaned in from Clementine's other

side. "Funny what the good Lord and a woman can do to change a man's attitude. Wouldn't you say, Harper?"

Harper fumbled a can of cream-of-mushroom soup. "Are you talking about Fergus?"

"And Joel." Marigold scooped up the can from the floor before Harper could and set it on the table. "Joel was never a curmudgeon, of course, but he was in a rut. Far too serious. But he's been smiling more since you came to town. Look at him."

As if she could stop looking at him. He seemed more than comfortable at the stove, his posture relaxed, his foot tapping a beat only he could hear, and oh, she shouldn't notice the way his broad shoulders and biceps flexed as he tended the stove. Then he flipped the sautéing strips of chicken with far more flourish and flair than Harper would ever dare. If she'd flicked chicken that high, it would've ended up on the floor.

Others cheered, Maude fisted her hands on her hips and Fergus ditched the pimientos to get a closer look. With a smile, Joel offered him the spatula.

Meanwhile, Marigold was staring at Harper. At once, the whole scene with the french fries came rushing back to her. Hadn't Joel mentioned Marigold had played matchmaker in the past?

Oh, dear.

"Could you pass the sour cream, please?"

Marigold pushed over the large container. "You temper him so well, Harper."

Clementine shook her head at her husband's grandmother. "Marigold, maybe Harper doesn't want you to play matchmaker for her."

"I'm not doing that at all." Marigold blinked, feigning innocence. "I learned my lesson with you and Liam."

Harper appreciated Clementine's intervention, but perhaps she should just switch the topic of conversation. "There, the sour cream is mixed in. What's next on the recipe?"

"Fine. I'll throw subtlety out the window and say it straight, then." Marigold tapped Harper's wrist. "I heard what Maude was saying about Adriana. Well, Adriana was a gem of a woman—sure as I'm standing here—but that doesn't mean she'd want Joel missing out on all the good the Lord has for him. Don't lose out on happiness because of the past."

She couldn't ignore the past, though. Which meant she couldn't envision the future. "Thanks, Marigold, but there's nothing between me and Joel, and there never will be."

Not with the secret she was keeping from him and everyone else in this town.

Chapter Fourteen

Returning to the recipe in front of her, Harper prayed for guidance. She reminded herself of the Bible verse about God's word being a lamp to her feet and a light to her path. But so far, He hadn't given her a clue what to do other than put one foot in front of the other.

Nevertheless, Marigold's words hit her somewhere deep within, nudging her to choose.

The rest of the time passed quickly, and soon the casseroles were labeled and tucked into the freezer in their foil packaging. Cleanup was quick under Maude's direction, and then everyone bade each other farewell and made their way from the church. Harper was walking out when she had no choice but to fall into step beside Joel.

"Hi." A lock of Joel's swooshy hair had fallen over his brow.

"Hi, yourself." She ignored the thrill she felt at his closeness. "Mighty fancy work at the stove, there."

"I told you I was a line cook in college."

She scoffed. "My mom's a chef, but she never tossed meat in the air."

"That's because she's a serious chef. I was a goofball. Still am. But hey."

Glowering, Maude held the kitchen door open for them, jangling the church keys.

Smiling an apology, Harper hurried out the door. "Where's Maisie?"

"She left with the Murphys."

She hadn't noticed. Then again, she hadn't been aware of much of anything except him and the turmoil in her chest. "Playdate?"

"More like they're watching her for me. I've got a meeting."

"If you ever need someone to watch Maisie, I'm more than happy to." Spending time with Maisie was precious. "She and I had a great time together while you were in the kitchen the other night."

Maude huffed past them, shaking her head, then got in her car, muttering. Joel rubbed his mouth like he was agitated.

"What did I miss? Maude seems upset, and you're not very happy right now, either."

Joel stared at the sidewalk at their feet. "I just

wish Maude hadn't overheard that you were at my house for dinner, that's all."

"Why?" Maybe it was silly to feel hurt like this when she was avoiding him, but was he ashamed of her? The pain in her gut felt an awful lot like rejection.

"Let's move to the patio." Joel led her to a bench beneath shady trees, where they'd be sheltered from the blazing sun but also away from the street and traffic noise. His posture was as rigid as hers as they sat side by side on a stone bench.

"Maude gave me an earful about Adriana in the kitchen. If she's upset because she thinks we're dating, well, there's nothing going on." Nothing beyond the war within her whenever he was around. But Maude didn't need to fear. "I'm no threat."

"Actually, you are."

Harper's breath stuck somewhere in her chest. "What are you talking about?"

"With me adopting Maisie." He stared at the ground. "Someone saw you hug me in front of DeLuca's, and Sebastian heard about it. His lawyer suggested that between Kjersti's marriage plot and you and me hugging, I've got a 'chaotic romantic life.' Not a good thing for Maisie to witness. And since your mom had a bit of a reputation in the past—"

She didn't let him finish. "My mom isn't like that now. And I'm not like Kjersti. I wasn't making moves on you, and I don't want anyone's money. I thought you were over thinking I was like that."

"I know. It's offensive, but Larry—the attorney—made a veiled threat that they'd use it against me in a custody hearing. I didn't tell anyone so they wouldn't be burdened. The rumors—"

"Are just that. Rumors. And hold up—you knew about this when you met Sebastian's attorney? That was how long ago, and you didn't tell me?"

His brow furrowed like tilled earth. "I didn't want to hurt you. I thought it was better to protect our reputations if we weren't ever in a position that could be interpreted as dating."

Her back teeth ground together. "You weren't thinking of my reputation, Joel."

"You're right. I'm sorry. I was thinking about mine, for Maisie's sake. And I feel bad for not being more gracious about your offer to watch Maisie just now, but you see why I can't allow that, right? It would give credence to that totally false rumor that I had something going with Kjersti. That I blur the line between romance and childcare."

"You feel bad." She snorted. "Of all the nerve. I would have understood."

"You're right. I'm sorry. None of what Sebastian's attorney said was true, but someone's been watching me and reporting things to Sebastian, probably through his aunt. Now Maude knows you had dinner at our house, and she'll probably tell someone." A muscle worked in his cheek. "I wish I knew who it was. They knew about Kjersti, they knew you hugged me—"

"Don't get too excited about that hug, Joel. I was thanking you. Nothing more."

"Believe me, I know." The sarcastic edge to his tone matched hers. "But I'm playing the game because I don't want to lose Maisie. I'm sorry."

"It's not like I want to date you, either, you arrogant…mountain of a human being," she blurted, annoyed she couldn't come up with a better zinger.

Was that pain flashing in his eyes? "Thanks for making that clear."

"I would never want to date someone who didn't defend my honor. My mom's honor." Why was she still talking? This was the most ridiculous conversation she'd ever had.

Ridiculous…but enlightening. She suddenly knew what she had to do with her life.

She stood up, staring at the Peace rosebushes behind Joel. "You won't need to worry about it much longer. I'm selling the grove and leaving Widow's Peak Creek."

He stood, too, eyes round. "But you've grown roots here. Made friends." For someone who didn't want anyone to think he might date her, he sure looked stricken.

Well, she was upset, too. "It's better for everyone."

"What about Trish? Maisie?"

"Maisie, who you don't even want me to babysit?"

"I'm sorry, okay? The custody thing has been such a mess I've handled things poorly. But people here care about you."

She noted he didn't mention himself.

It was just as well.

But maybe she should be honest with him, too, before she left. "It's not about you." Not entirely, anyway. "Doug Davis is my father, okay?"

His jaw went slack. "Harper, that's—"

"Unbelievable? Yeah, I know, but I got the DNA results. Trish is my aunt. I tried to figure out if there were any other scenarios to make that possible, but Doug was the only viable option. So I visited him. He got so upset, I almost gave him a heart attack."

"That cardiac episode? It's been a week, and you didn't tell me you found out who your dad is?"

She wouldn't point out the irony of him getting upset that she'd kept a secret from him. "My mom confirmed it, but I still don't have the whole story. So there you go. Adriana was my half sister. Maisie is my niece. And if it goes public, Trish would be devastated and Doug might have a bad heart attack. It's a lot easier if I just leave town while no one's the wiser."

Harper was leaving.

It felt like a blow on top of a bruise. Joel still wasn't over the shock that she was Doug's daughter. He could only imagine the emotions expressed on his face: Surprise. Astonishment. Disbelief.

They were nothing compared to the stricken look marring Harper's features. He wished he could pull her into his arms to comfort her, get some comfort *from* her, but he shoved his hands into his front pockets instead.

"You'd leave even though Doug is here? You have so much to talk about."

She scoffed. "He told me to go away, Joel."

That couldn't be true. "Doug can hardly speak, and if he could, he wouldn't—"

"He did. It took considerable effort, but he said, 'Go away.'"

A memory surfaced in Joel's brain. When he had introduced Harper to Doug for the first time, Doug scowled. It hadn't originated with her entrance into his room. That meant it wasn't because he thought Joel had brought a girlfriend to meet him.

Doug's glower began the moment he'd introduced her as Sheila Price's daughter.

That meant Doug had known who Harper was. That she was his child. One would think a man with a long-lost daughter would have broken down in lament over missing every moment of her life until now.

Or smiled and reached for her, glad to meet her for the first time.

Instead, Doug had iced over.

Joel could buy that Doug had been in shock at seeing her for the first time. But when she'd visited him in private, he told her to go away? It was unfathomable. How could his father-in-law have rejected Harper—not just thirty years ago but again at Creekside Retirement Village, when she was standing in front of him?

Rage coursed through Joel's veins. This didn't happen often, but when it did, he made a bee-line for the gym to punch a bag before he took his anger out on something else.

Later. He had to be here for Harper now.

"I'm so sorry. It shouldn't have happened like this. None of it."

"I came here for answers, didn't I? I got what I wanted. Sort of. My mom has promised to explain everything to me in person, but it's not hard to put it together. It's interesting, though. I always thought my father was an immature guy who got scared by the responsibility of an unexpected baby. But Doug wasn't a callow kid. He was a stable single dad. It doesn't make sense that he would have left my mom on her own."

Joel wouldn't have thought so, but that look in Doug's eyes at the retirement village was one of anger. Fear, even. "You need answers from your mom."

"No matter what she has to say, though, it's best that I leave. I made peace a long time ago with the possibility that I'd never be part of my father's life. Maybe even that he had another family." She looked at him, her eyes almost vacant. "It turns out he had the world's most perfect family."

"No one's family is perfect, Harper."

"His sure sounds like it. He's a town favorite. So is Adriana. No one can ever know about this, okay, Joel? It would cause too much hurt."

As if her leaving wouldn't cause pain? Joel had no right to ask her to stay, but panic rose in his chest. It felt like everything he wanted was slipping away and he was powerless to stop it.

He'd honor her request, though. "I'll keep your secret."

"I gave you such a hard time about children

learning about their fathers. Remember? But finding mine has only opened a can of worms."

"I took your words to heart, though. Since Sebastian hasn't backed down on the petition for shared custody, I realized I'd have to tell Maisie about him sooner or later. To that end, I asked if she had any questions about him. It doesn't sound like much, but it's a step. In the meantime, I decided it might be helpful to me to observe him when she's nearby, to see how he acts when she's close. Will he be engaged or indifferent? I've set up an in-person meeting with him. No lawyers, just us. I don't intend for him and Maisie to meet, but if they do, I'm trusting God will be in the midst of it."

"That's huge, Joel. When?"

"In less than an hour. Clementine and Liam are bringing the kids to the park to play, and Sebastian and I will be at one of the picnic benches."

Her hand went to her mouth. "Are you okay?"

"I'm not sure, to be honest." He cracked his knuckles, still needing to vent some of the rage in his system. "I can't help thinking the worst of him. But I need to do this for Maisie."

"I think that's a good plan." She looked conflicted, as if she wanted to support him but wasn't sure how.

"I'd probably better get going." He had one

more stop to make, and he also wanted time to pray beforehand. God held Maisie in His capable hands, and Joel had to trust Him.

But trusting Him seemed a lot harder when it had to do with his daughter than anything else he'd faced in his life.

"I'll be praying. Will you let me know how it goes?"

"Of course." But not by text. In person. She might be leaving town, but he didn't feel like this conversation was finished.

Joel parked his truck in front of Maude's house, where he found her trimming the rosebushes lining the walkway. Lips pursed like a string-tie bag, she dropped her clippers into the pocket of her gardening apron. "You don't have your girlfriend with you?"

"I don't have a girlfriend, Maude."

"That's what you told me, but it's not true. She said you had dinner at your house."

"Technically, yes, but Trish invited us to dinner and had car trouble. I had to host at the last minute. That doesn't make Harper my girlfriend. I haven't dated anyone since Adriana."

"Now that's a bald-faced lie, Joel. You dumped Kjersti, so she couldn't work for you anymore."

"I didn't *dump* her. I terminated her employment because she wanted Maisie's inheritance."

This was the first time he'd seen Maude flustered. "No, she said you two had a future, and then you called it off."

"She lied. Another thing, Maude—but you witnessed Adriana signing the trust for Maisie, right? You're one of only a few people in town who knows Maisie gets a monthly stipend." That was confidential information, but he wouldn't go into that now. "I'm guessing you told someone all of those things. And maybe you saw Harper hug me outside DeLuca's and talked about that, too."

"I don't deny it." Her jaw worked. "But everyone in the beauty parlor agreed with me that you're not honoring Adriana's memory, cavorting with women who can't hold a candle to her. You've changed, and I don't like it."

He'd changed? Joel brushed the charge aside for the moment. "I'm sure you didn't mean to, but you started a rumor, and now Sebastian's lawyer is making false claims about me and Kjersti and even Harper. It could hurt my chances of adopting Maisie."

"I don't want that snake getting his hands on Maisie or her money, but I don't know how Sebastian would've heard it anyway. He wasn't in the beauty parlor."

"Sebastian's aunt still lives in town, doesn't she? She's never wanted a relationship with

Maisie, but I'm sure she's kept in touch with Sebastian. Someone must've told her. You know how gossip spreads. Like ink in water. And now it could come out in court."

"*I* did that?" Maude's eyes started streaming. She wiped them with her sleeve. "I just didn't want you to forget Adriana."

"That could never happen."

"Sure seems like it."

"It's not like that." What had Harper called him? An arrogant mountain of a person? She'd been completely flustered when she'd thrown that at him. He bit back a smile. "Anyway, thanks for being honest with me, Maude."

"I didn't mean to gossip, but it's like the whole world forgets people when they pass... Them and their friends."

Was that what this was about? "You feel forgotten?"

"Odell moved away, didn't he?" Her tears fell in earnest now. "My only child and he's too busy for me. Everyone's too busy for me. No one needs me for advice or help or to set them up in matches the way Marigold does. I'm alone and..."

Lonely. Joel's gut cinched tight. "You're right when you said I've changed. Between me worrying about Sebastian trying to get custody of Maisie and, yes, Harper, I haven't had a mind for much of anything else. Or anyone. Adriana would be shaking her head at me for being so self-absorbed." He reached out to hug her. "I'm sorry I haven't been a better friend."

"I don't' know why you'd want to be my friend after I was such a blabbermouth. If that man gets custody of Maisie—"

"It's in God's hands, but I'm going to talk to him about it. Right now." He squeezed her shoulders before letting her go. "You matter to me. To this town. We love you, Maude. But love grows—it doesn't divide. There's more than enough room for new friends in both of our lives."

He left Maude with a promise to have dinner together soon and headed to the park. He prayed he'd be a better friend to those who were lonely around him, but right now, it was time to face Sebastian.

Chapter Fifteen

Sebastian was late. Joel swung a leg over the picnic table bench so he had a better view of the parking lot.

He had never met Sebastian, but he recalled Adriana's descriptions of him: dark hair, trim build. Joel kept watch while looking every few moments at the three children playing on the swing set fifty-odd yards away. Their shrieks and giggles carried on the breeze, as did snatches of Liam's and Clementine's occasional shouts of encouragement or laughter.

Joel didn't have a plan for today, but he was convinced this would be the best way to talk. He owed Clementine and Liam big-time for their help with this today and for their help with Maisie the past few weeks.

Lord, I have so much to be grateful for. In these stressful moments, I lose sight of my blessings, don't I? Forgive me.

It was hard not to think about Harper right now, too. Parting the way they had felt terrible, but he had to let it go for the moment.

Let it go. Such a hard thing to do since he felt more in control when he could grip his worries tightly; but it was necessary to empty his hands so God could use them as He wished.

Here you go, Lord. Maisie. Harper. My life. Everything. Help me to keep on giving them all to You when I want to snatch them back.

A dark-haired man in sunglasses, jeans and a too-tight button-down strolled into the park, cell phone in hand.

"Sebastian?" Joel stood up, and the man's head jerked, as if he was taken aback by Joel's size. Joel didn't relish the fact that he'd intimidated Sebastian physically, for it wasn't his physique that concerned God but his heart. All he wanted was for God to be pleased with him, and he hoped today would help him do what was best for Maisie.

Joel stuck out his hand. "I'm Joel Morgan."

"Sebastian Green." The sour odors of stale alcohol and tobacco wafted around him. "Where's Maisie?"

"Playing." Joel tipped his head toward the kids. "Thanks for meeting me so we could talk. Dad to dad, no lawyers."

"Except *you're* a lawyer."

"It's just a conversation." Joel gestured at the

picnic table. As they sat down, he prayed for guidance. "She's had a lot of changes in the past two years. If you're determined to take this to court, you and I both need to understand how this will affect her. So I've decided to consult with a child psychologist. I want Maisie to feel as safe and secure as possible—"

Sebastian's phone beeped. He removed his sunglasses and looked at it, his brow furrowing. "Changes, yeah, since Adriana."

What had Adriana ever seen in this guy? He must have been a lot more charming back in the day...before it had become clear he just wanted her money.

"If you're serious about knowing Maisie, why not start with visitation?"

Rolling his bloodshot eyes, Sebastian returned to his phone, swiping his finger back and forth. "Come on, dude. I drove all the way from San Francisco because I thought you said you were ready to negotiate."

"I never used the word *negotiate*. I said 'discuss.'" Joel fought to keep his cool. "And I'd think the drive was worth it to observe your daughter. She's not ready to meet you, but you can see her right there."

At last, Sebastian's gaze fixed on the three kids playing together. "She hasn't stopped moving. Is she always that energetic? Screaming?"

Nothing about how cute she was, just his surprise at how kids ran around playgrounds? "What can I say?"

Sebastian chuckled. "Look at her, going up the slide the wrong way."

Joel's chest tightened. "Not the girl in pink. See the girl in yellow? *That's* Maisie."

Sebastian grimaced. "With the glasses?"

"Yes. The girl in pink just turned five. Maisie is eight."

"Five, eight—it's all the same."

Hardly, but Joel let the comment slip by. "See how happy she is? Uprooting her would cause a lot of angst. This is where her friends are, her doctors, her vision therapist—"

"Doctors, as in plural?" Sebastian's focus lifted from his phone. "She's sick?" There wasn't concern in his voice. More like annoyance.

"Not sick, but she was a preemie and has asthma, so they keep an eye on that. The vision therapist is for her amblyopia. She's doing great but still needs a little more work on her binocular vision." Joel shifted so he could better watch Maisie.

"I'd have to be the one to take her to those appointments, huh?" His red-rimmed eyes glazed over.

Joel caught a glimpse of the screen. Looked like an online card game of some sort. "Adriana told me you had a problem with gambling. Looks like it might still be a big part of your life, eh, Sebastian?"

He slammed the phone facedown. "Look, she's *my* daughter, and if you fight me on it in open court, it could get ugly for you."

"For Maisie, you mean. Having to endure a bitter dispute like that. I don't care about me, but she's a child. She's never even met you. Did you ever think about what this could do to her?"

"You brought up a therapist. You've got a lot of money lying around from her inheritance, so you can pay for it."

Sebastian had just played into Joel's hands. "Where'd you get the idea that Maisie has an inheritance?"

"Come on, man, it's common knowledge. One of Adriana's friends witnessed her signing the documents."

"Yeah, Maude didn't do the greatest job keeping that confidential."

"You admit there's money."

"Yes, but it's Maisie's."

"She's a minor. It goes to whoever is in charge of her."

Disgust churned in Joel's stomach. He wished he'd been wrong about Sebastian, but if the man had wanted a relationship with Maisie, money would have had nothing to do with this discussion.

Joel, on the other hand, would give everything he owned for Maisie. His home, his savings, his life.

"Look, if it's money you want, nothing will stop you from pursuing this. But if you insist on this going before a judge, I will testify you didn't recognize your own daughter today and you'd been drinking recently. If you want a relationship with Maisie, you'd put her and her needs first. And clean up your act."

Sebastian's phone had all his attention. "I'm not hungover."

"You reek of alcohol." Joel's spine stiffened. "And you've been on a gambling app since you got here. I will testify to those things in court—not to shame you but because I don't think Maisie is your concern at all. I've been the man in Maisie's life since she was tiny. Her sole parent for the past two years. The one who knows the names of all her stuffed animals and the one who taught her to ride a bike. The one who nurses her when she gets sick and takes her to church and, with the support of loving friends and family, has the privilege to watch her grow."

"But—"

"But you're listed on her birth certificate, so you think that gives you all the power? I'm in family law, so I'm aware judges factor blood relationships into their decisions about custody.

They also consider the child's welfare, and I am certain you won't get what you want based on what's known in court as *abandonment*. You've never given her a dime. Never had her in your home or visited hers. And you aren't remotely curious about her now when she's just yards away."

He glanced over at her, playing with the kids. Liam and Clementine didn't hide their curiosity, though, watching Joel's exchange with Sebastian. "I'll also tell the judge about the suspicious timing of your suit, coinciding with the rumor about Maisie's inheritance."

"You won't say that on the record. Somehow, someday, Maisie could find out and she'd be a wreck."

Harper's sad eyes were fresh in his mind as he looked at Sebastian.

"She would find out. You're right. Because much as I want to protect her, I don't lie to her."

Sebastian's attention returned to his phone.

Angry as he was, Joel's heart broke at the bigger picture of what was happening here. "I'm willing to pay for therapy for your gambling addiction."

"I'm not addicted," Sebastian yelled, then rubbed his hair, mussing the structured style.

"You're indebted to someone?" As he had been when he came into Adriana's life?

"Maybe," he hedged. "That's what you want to hear, right? And you're offering to pay for addiction therapy so I'll go away, right? Or to blackmail me."

"No, to help you. Not with Maisie's money, but mine. I'm not threatening you, Sebastian, but Maisie deserves better than to be subjected to a court battle you won't win. The court will see as well as I can that you are not in it for her. Not up to your eyeballs in addiction. You need to put Maisie first and get back on track. God has a better existence in store for you than this."

Sebastian's eyes were glued to his phone, but they looked watery. Were they tears or the after-effects from drinking and staring at a screen?

Then he blinked. "What have I done?"

Joel didn't understand. Was Sebastian talking about the gambling app? Or Maisie?

"Daddy!"

Joel stood. He knew Maisie's cry anywhere. He ran toward the playground, heart pounding in fear as Maisie lay in a heap beneath the jungle gym.

To his immense relief, she pushed up from the ground as the others reached her. In a moment, she was in his arms. "Bug, are you okay?"

"I fell on my knees." Her words came out through tears.

"Are they scratched up?"

"I don't know." She looked down.

She'd scraped both knees, but they'd heal quickly. "Let's go wash you up and get bandages." Joel exchanged a small smile with Clementine and Liam.

"You can put me down, Daddy. I'm okay now."

He dutifully set her on the ground. "Why don't you get your things?" She'd brought a small backpack with her.

No worse for the wear, she ran off with the kids to where Liam and Clementine had been sitting on a bench.

"How'd it go?" Liam's voice was low. "Did Sebastian back off before he left?"

Left? Joel spun around. Sure enough, the picnic bench where they'd been sitting was vacant. Sebastian had disappeared.

"I don't know what's going to happen, to be honest, but I gave it my best shot."

Maisie returned, pouting. "I forgot, Daddy. We were going to look for ducks on the creek."

"I have a first aid kit," Clementine said. "I can clean those boo-boos and we can look at ducks, and you can pick her up at our house later."

"Are you sure?" They'd had her a long time—but then again, he really wanted to talk to Harper some more.

"Yes," Maisie answered the same time as Clementine.

"Okay, then." He kissed her atop the head. "See you soon, Bug. Say hi to the ducks for me."

"Quack," she said, waving.

Joel ambled toward the parking lot, wondering where Sebastian had gone. To his surprise, he didn't feel afraid, only hopeful—even though there would be challenges in the future. Whether Sebastian continued to fight for custody or let Joel adopt her, either way, Maisie would learn more about Sebastian. She'd be hurt that he hadn't wanted her until she was eight and an heiress, and Joel hated that.

But he'd be there when it happened to help patch her broken heart. She would never know a day without Joel's love, and he could only pray that it would be enough to soothe the sting.

Harper strolled down the dirt path cut between two rows of olive trees near the house. Today, her emotions had bounced through her heart and mind like pinballs, haphazard and dizzying. She'd desperately needed a few minutes to collect herself, and being out here, deeply breathing in the fresh air, had a calming effect on her.

Just like it had on her grandfather, according to Joel.

Her burgeoning sense of calm fled the moment Joel's truck turned into the driveway. How had it gone with Sebastian? She jogged over to meet him on the driveway, watching his face for clues, but then she realized the back seat was empty.

Panic struck her heart. The instant he got out of the truck, she grabbed his sleeve. "Where's Maisie? Sebastian didn't show up with a court order or something so he could take her?"

"No, not that at all." He took reassuring hold of her upper arms. "I didn't mean to scare you. She's still with the Murphys. I don't know what's going to happen, but I laid it on the line. I wanted him to put her first. Unfortunately, I'm not sure I made any headway. I'm confident he has a gambling addiction, maybe alcohol, too. He wants that money."

"What a fool he is." She should pity him, but it wasn't easy. "The greatest treasure isn't Maisie's bank account. It's her."

"She fell at the park, and his first instinct wasn't to rush to her. It was to run away. He left without a word." His hands fell from her shoulders. "Someday Maisie will want to know more, and I'll have to tell her the truth, just like you said. No matter how much it gets sugarcoated, she will realize her father didn't want her until he learned she had money. I wish I could protect her from it, but I can't."

That was his greatest fear, wasn't it? That he couldn't protect those under his care?

"You can't protect her from that pain, but you

can walk alongside her on that path. Show her how to rely on God's help."

The furrows in his brow smoothed a fraction. "You're right, Harper. You were right about so many things. There's so much to tell you. I was thinking—"

An unfamiliar car pulled into her driveway. "Maybe they're lost and need directions." She walked toward the slowing car, smiling at the strange white-haired man in the driver's seat. But then a woman exited the back seat, the sun giving her blond hair a red-gold sheen.

"Mom? What are you doing here?"

"Surprise!" Her mother ran straight into Harper's arms.

Oh, it felt good to hug her. Things were strained between them, and Harper couldn't pretend she was okay with how their last conversation had gone. But she loved her mother. Always had, always will.

"I'd better get my things from the cab." Her mom turned back to the car, but Joel was already getting her bags from the trunk. When he was clear, they waved goodbye to the driver.

Harper smiled at Joel. "This is my mother, Sheila Price. Mom, this is Joel Morgan, my... friend and your dad's law partner."

"Sheila." He offered his hand. "I thought you were in Europe for another week at least."

"I'm supposed to be, but I'd much rather be with Harper right now. There's a lot to discuss."

"I'll let you get to it, then. But while you're in town, Sheila, if you have a few minutes to talk about your dad's estate, that'd be great. Harper knows how to contact me."

"I suspect you're much busier than I, so why not call me when your schedule allows? Here." She reached into her purse and pulled out a card. "This has my phone and email on it. But before you leave, I'm so sorry about Adriana. She was a lovely girl. I wish Harper could have known her."

"I feel a little like I did, through others' stories about her. And I've seen her photo." On Maisie's nightstand.

"She would have loved Harper. I'm sure of it." Joel smiled, but she could see hurt in his eyes. "She would've loved a sister."

"Ah, so Harper told you." Mom's lips twisted, but it was hard to read her expression.

"Only Joel. No one else."

Nodding, Mom eyed Joel. "I appreciate you sending letters to tell me about my father. I didn't get them until today. I scheduled a layover in Phoenix so I could stop by the apartment, and there they were, in the stack of mail collected by our neighbor Mrs. Teegarden while Harper has been here."

That made no sense to Harper. "But they were mailed months apart. They both arrived in the past few weeks while I was in California? That doesn't make sense." Harper wanted to believe her mother, but she was certain Joel wouldn't buy a word of this. He probably thought her mom had received the letters and never opened them until today.

In any case, it was hard to read his expression.

Her mom sighed, pulling two envelopes out of her purse. Thick, white business-sized envelopes with the Morgan & Price Law Firm return address stamped in the upper-left corner, but that was about the only part of the envelope still visible. Stickers and pen markings covered the front. "They're a confusing mess, but the original address is still there if you peel the sticker off. The numbers of our street address were transposed, and it looks like it took the postal service a while to straighten it out."

"Transposed?" Joel's eyes narrowed, taking an envelope her mom offered.

"The sixes and the eights got mixed up on both letters."

Harper peered over his shoulder. Sure enough, the street address was wrong on the computer-printed address. She could see it plain as day, as well as several postmarks—one from just days ago. "I knew we didn't get the letters, but I'm shocked this is what happened."

Joel's shoulders sagged. "It's entirely my fault, too. Right after Clark passed, Shirley—the administrative assistant—took personal leave for her husband's surgery, so I'm the one who found your address online. I'm the one who jotted it down on a piece of paper and then later entered it into our database. I clearly did it incorrectly. I'm so sorry."

Mom waved her hand in dismissal. "It could've been listed incorrectly online."

"I doubt it because I did the same thing with two case files that week." Joel rubbed his hand over his mouth. "I was under a lot of stress after Clark passed. Still, there's no excuse."

"Grief is an excuse," Harper said.

"Not an excuse for my attitude. I accused you two of having those letters and disregarding them. I was so bullheaded. So suspicious of you both and sharp-tongued. I wish I could take it back. I'm so sorry."

It took strength to own up to his mistake and apologize, but it was one more testament to Joel's character. Harper wasn't angry about it, though. In fact, she hadn't been angry about their first meeting for a long time. Not since she understood how deep his need to protect his loved ones went. "It's okay. Honest. I understand why you were concerned. I'm just sorry it happened."

"Ultimately, the responsibility for this mess is mine," Mom said, her voice wavering. "None of this would have happened if I'd reconciled with my dad. I'd like to explain what happened between me and my dad, if I could. To both of you."

He held up a hand. "You don't owe me anything, Sheila."

"I know it's one-sided coming from me, but you were close to him. I'd be relieved to tell you."

So this was it. The truth at last.

Harper took a deep breath and prayed for peace.

Chapter Sixteen

God answered Harper's prayer, and with a sense of calm filling her, she met Joel's concerned gaze. "Please stay, Joel."

After a moment, he nodded, then gestured at the porch. "Do you want to sit down?"

"No, it won't take long, and I've been on a plane or in a car all day anyway." Mom shoved her hands into her pockets. "Dad and I grieved my mom's death differently. He served others to relieve his pain, but I fed my grief, stewing in anger. I didn't realize his acts of community service made him feel better, though. We didn't go to church, so I believed him to be a hypocrite, motivated by making himself look good in others' eyes."

Harper thought back over several conversations she'd had with folks in town. "But Clark went to church."

"He did," Joel said. "But I don't think he started attending until ten or fifteen years ago."

"I'm glad we shared a faith, even though we didn't know it." Mom swiped a lone tear. "Back then, though, you'd never have thought I would become a believer. Let's just say I was not the most well-behaved teenager at Widow's Peak Creek High, and my behavior didn't improve much when I was in my early twenties."

Troublemaker had been Maude's word.

"Anyway," Mom continued, "I lied. A lot. Right before high school graduation, I snuck out my window to meet some girlfriends. We toilet papered the principal's house—don't look at me like that, Harper. I told you I didn't use the best judgment back then."

"Sorry. It's just I've never heard any of this." And her mom had been so strict with her.

"My dad caught me climbing back through my bedroom window, and of course he wanted to know where I'd been and what I was doing. I didn't want my friends to get in trouble, so I lied and said I was out toilet papering someone's house with a kid in my class named Marty Hughes."

Harper's gasp dried her throat. "He's Rowena's nephew, isn't he?"

Mom's eyes sparked. "You know Rowena?"

"Am I named for her, Mom?"

"Yes, sweetheart—but I'll finish the story before we talk about her. Anyway, I blamed Marty for a reason. The week before, he'd cheated off my math test, but when the teacher noted our identical exams, Marty told the teacher that *I* was the one stealing *his* answers. Guess which one of us got the automatic failing grade on the test?"

"Ouch." Joel winced.

"It wasn't fair, but my dad didn't do anything to back me up. He was so nice to everyone, believed the best of everyone—except for me, I guess. I wanted him to get mad at Marty over something since he didn't support me when it came to the math test, so I lied about being with Marty."

"Uh-oh." Harper could see where this was going.

"My dad went straight over to confront the Hughes family over it. Turns out Marty was in the ER with food poisoning when I said he was with me, toilet papering the principal's house. So it was obvious I'd lied. Dad was mortified that I'd caused a strain in his relationship with an upstanding family in town. And he didn't quite trust me after that. I don't blame him. I lived at home as a college student, working odd jobs—"

"Like helping Rowena," Harper interrupted.

"Just like that." Mom's smile softened at the second mention of Rowena's name. "She was kind to me, despite what most people thought of me in town. Then, when I was twenty-two, I met Doug in the pasta section of the market. We both reached for lasagna noodles and got to talking." Mom shrugged. "He wanted our relationship kept quiet—I thought so his ex-wife wouldn't want more alimony or something. He was always complaining about her. I was madly in love, and I thought we'd get married. When I went to tell him I was pregnant, though, he wasn't alone. There was another woman with him. It turns out he had a string of us, all secrets. None of us knew about the others, and he had no intention of getting married again because he didn't want anyone else to get a share of his money. Doug had such a radiant reputation—a generous donor, a mayor in the making, the greatest thing since milk chocolate. Like my dad's exterior, it was all a shell for others to admire. But in private? He wasn't generous with me. He threw me out and threatened that if I told anyone about him, he'd inform everyone I was a lying… Well, I won't tell you the rest. But he was the amazing Doug Davis—why would anyone believe me? So I didn't lie when I told you I never knew your father well, Harper. I thought I did, but in truth, he was a stranger to me."

"Oh, Mom." Harper's mind was all over the place. Doug had known all about her and sent her and her mom away to protect his reputation and his bank account. "I'm so sorry."

"Naturally, I told my dad," Mom continued. "He believed I was pregnant but not with Doug's baby."

"Clark figured you named Doug as a way to seek revenge, like you'd done with Marty?" Joel's voice was soft.

Mom nodded. "Dad didn't want to 'ruin another friendship' over my lies. In fact, he said I brought shame to him. He wanted the name of Price to mean something good in this town."

"So you ran away." Harper reached for her mom's hand.

"I reached out once, to tell him you'd been born. But he didn't write back."

Joel shook his head. "He sent letters for years."

"Starting when Harper was around five, yes."

Joel's eyes narrowed as he did the math. "Twenty-five years ago. That's when Clark accepted God."

Harper's hand went to her mouth. "He must have wanted to reconcile with you, Mom."

"I was so hurt he didn't respond when I told him about Harper, I didn't open his letters when he finally wrote to me." She wiped a lone tear from her cheek. "I told you we didn't have family because I believed that…we didn't anymore."

Harper squeezed her mom's hand, hard. "That's heartbreaking."

"What's heartbreaking is he died believing that the last time I spoke to him, I lied to him."

Joel stared squarely at Sheila. "He loved you. That's the most important thing, and I hope you don't forget it. He regretted his words to you—I'm sure of it because he reached out to you and left something for both of you. He passed away loving you."

"Thank you for that, Joel. And for listening. Sometime, I'd love to ask you more about my dad's later years if you're inclined. He clearly changed a lot. I mean, an olive grove?" Mom looked around the trees and waggled her eyebrows.

"Sure, but for now, I'll let you two talk. I need to get my daughter, anyway." His soulful gaze met Harper's. "My work schedule is light this week, so I'm available most anytime."

She understood his message. He wasn't just referring to having time to speak with her mother about Clark. He wanted to talk to Harper.

Alone.

But what more was there to say? Nothing could change the facts. Doug was her father, and she'd initially wanted to keep that secret to protect his loved ones and his reputation, because she thought her mom had chosen not to tell him about Harper. Besides, she didn't want to cause him so much stress he could suffer another cardiac episode.

But now that she knew he'd never wanted her, the secret made her feel even worse. She was wrapped in shame over the whole thing. No wonder her mom had run away.

"I'll let you know, but I'm not sure how long Mom will be here, so…" She purposely let her sentence trail off. It was weak, blaming the uncertainty of her mother's plans on her inability to talk, but she didn't want to drag her mom into this.

"Okay." His eyes said he understood her unspoken message, too. "Have a good evening, and I look forward to chatting later, Sheila."

Once Joel drove away, Harper expected her mom to say something about the olive trees or wanting to see the house, but instead she pierced her with a look. "Is there something going on with Joel?"

"No." Never would be. "I mean, we're friends now, but he thought I came to get my hands on Clark's inheritance. It wasn't pretty at first."

"I can't blame him for making that assumption, considering I never reached out to him."

She tipped her head at the house. "Would you mind if we ran into town? The time change has me wanting dinner sooner rather than later, but I think we should make a stop first."

"Sure, I just need to go in and grab my purse. Where do you want to stop? Did you forget to pack something?"

"It's not that. I want to run by the retirement village. I never talked frankly with my father, and I regret it now. I don't want the same thing to happen to you. I think we should—"

"No way. I tried it once, and he almost had a heart attack. I don't want that to happen again—and besides, I'm not interested."

In her years of wondering about her father's identity, she'd known he'd hurt her mom. When she had started going to church, she realized she needed to forgive her father, to let go of any resentment or anger she felt toward him.

But now? She had a whole new level of anger bubbling inside her.

"We're not going to give him a heart attack, Harper. But the past thirty years have taught me you can't run away from your past. If I'm ever going to move on—if *we're* ever going to—I think we must at least talk to Doug. You say he can't speak, but I'm hopeful he can tell us something in another way. Or at least listen to what we have to say."

If she said no, denying her mother and herself this opportunity, would she look back with regret?

I'm not ready for this. Not sure I'll ever be.

Sending up a wordless prayer, Harper nodded. "I'll get my keys."

A few minutes later, Harper's ankles wobbled as she walked into Creekside Retirement Village. Thankfully, she had her mother's hand to cling to as they found their way to Doug's wing.

Harper had been praying since the decision was made to visit Doug, and even though she felt afraid, she had quickly come to believe her mom was probably right. Talking to Doug was the best place to start toward healing, whatever form that took. She didn't know God's plans— for her or her mom, or Doug, for that matter— but she had to trust Him.

I'm glad You're with me wherever I go, Lord.

She curled her trembling fingers into a soft fist and rapped on Doug's half-open door. "Mr. Davis?" She led her mom inside.

He sat in the same chair where he'd been last time, groomed and neat, an e-reader in his lap. He looked up with an eager expression, but his smile fell, replaced by a scowl. Just like their previous meetings.

"Hello, Doug. It's me, Sheila." Mom strode over. "Harper and I would like to talk to you. Five minutes is all I ask, but if you don't want us here, we'll go."

Harper waited for him to wave his hand, turn away—anything to indicate that they should go. But to her surprise, he didn't move. Mom clearly interpreted his inaction as assent, so she took the other chair. Harper dropped onto the window ledge as Maisie had done. Doug looked guarded and uncomfortable, but at least he was allowing them this moment.

This is what I always wanted, Lord, isn't it? To be with both my parents? But not quite like this.

Doug's throat and jaw worked. "What do you want?" His words were not clear and had obviously taken considerable effort to express.

"Nothing," Mom said.

His eyes narrowed. Then he shoved the e-reader closer to Harper, pointing a slender finger at the screen.

She scanned the words of the book he'd been reading—a mystery, maybe, because the section he was pointing out was about a motive for murder. Something about blackmail. *Oh...*

"Blackmail?" She leaned forward. "You think we want to blackmail you? We want your money? In exchange for what, our silence?"

Doug's nod was more of a jut of his chin. "How much?"

It took Harper a moment to not only understand his speech but to also realize he was asking how much money it would take for them to keep quiet about their relationship to him. Her father's first-ever words to her weren't just unfriendly, they were cruelly suspicious. It made her heart sink.

"Oh, Doug." Her mom shook her head. "I didn't want your money thirty years ago, and I don't want it now."

"Neither of us want it," Harper added. "All I ever wanted was to know who you were."

He looked away, lips downturned.

"I loved you, Doug. Not your money." Mom watched for an answer from him, but he gave none. "All I want now, though, is to tell you I forgive you for how you treated me—me and our daughter—thirty years ago."

He grunted.

Harper's heart still ached but for an altogether different reason than it had a moment ago. "I don't want anything *from* you, but I do want something *for* you. I'll be praying for you to find God. And hopefully value the people in your life. Even if I'm never one of those people."

Unlike Harper, her mom wasn't teary. She

was beaming. "Look how beautiful she is, Doug. Inside and out."

Warmth flooded Harper's chest, and she found herself smiling, too.

Doug's jaw was set in a hard, angry line. What was he thinking? Feeling? She waited for him to indicate a desire for her to stay, but after a minute, she rose, completely at peace.

"One last thing. I don't intend to advertise that you're my father, but I can't guarantee no one will ever find out. Joel knows the truth, and I'm going to tell him I'd like to be part of Maisie's life. I'm not sure what that will look like since I'm leaving town. But if you wish, you can reach out to me at any time. I'll come. That's all I have to say. I'll leave you two alone now." Harper watched for her mom's nod, and then she stepped out into the hallway.

Within five minutes, her mom had joined her. She looked tired, but her shoulders were relaxed and there was a softness to her countenance that said she had come to a similar place of inner rest that Harper had found.

Her mom took her hand. "Why don't we get takeout and eat on your porch? It's been a long day."

It had indeed.

Arm in arm with her mom, they left Doug behind them.

Would they ever come back? Would he reach out to Harper someday, curious to know her? She wasn't sure. But she would never stop praying for him to find peace in God.

Chapter Seventeen

The evening's dinner of takeout on the porch had been perfect for Harper and her mom—restful—and it gave them the privacy to talk about the past. Harper's stomach was full, but her curiosity was far from satisfied as she shut her to-go box from Del's. "You were so young, Mom. I don't know how you made it through, taking care of me."

"My love for you was fierce, that's how." Mom's eyes lost focus as she gazed at the Arbequina trees. "No, there's more to it than that. I can see where God took care of me, even though I didn't know Him yet. He was patient, and I'm convinced He sent people to help me along the way."

"Like the couple who gave you your first restaurant job." Harper had heard the story about the couple who had gotten her mom back into church. "The Riccis."

"The Riccis," Mom agreed. "I thought I'd work for them forever, but then they moved to be closer to their children. It was frightening, wondering what I'd do next. But that's when the job opened up for me in Tucson, and we moved there. The woman next door used to cook too much food and share leftovers with me. It took me a long time to figure out she was doing it on purpose. Every time we moved, people like that crossed our paths, didn't they?"

"They were blessings." Harper couldn't remember living in Tucson, but she'd heard the stories, and she certainly knew what life had been like in her growing-up years. They hadn't put down roots anywhere, but that didn't meant they hadn't made friends.

Mom shifted on the noisy wicker love seat they were sharing. "I haven't been a blessing in anyone's life like that, that I know of."

"That's not true. You are a generous, giving person, Mom."

"But I'd like to do more. Formal-like, you know?"

"How so?"

Mom sipped her chocolate milkshake. "I haven't the foggiest. I just took all those specialized culinary courses on the cruise, so maybe they'll factor in somehow."

Harper recognized her mom's joking tone,

but there was something to it. "Will you open your own restaurant?"

"I'm not sure I can see myself managing one." Mom finished off her last french fry. "But teaching culinary skills appeals to me. Something that reaches out to young people who were like I was. On their own, in need of a hand up." She clasped her palms together on her lap. "I'll ask God what He thinks."

"That's a good place to start." Harper took a sip of her lemon-lime soda. "I want in, whatever it turns out to be. Wherever. But I assume we're going back to Phoenix."

"You could leave all this?" Mom took a deep breath. "It's so beautiful. So quiet."

Harper wouldn't dispute that. When she'd first arrived, she'd thought the area to be lovely, but she'd been hesitant to embrace it because of her mother's past experiences here. "There's a lot of baggage in Widow's Peak Creek, though, Mom."

"Doug, you mean? Don't let him stop you from enjoying the closeness of family here, if you decide that's what you want."

Family. Maisie and Trish. Thinking of them hurt her heart.

"The truth is, there is a little something with Joel." She took a big breath. "Not a *big* something. And it's only on my side. In fact, he said dating—me, in particular—could hurt his chances of adopting Maisie because her biological dad's lawyer gave him a hard time about… Well, it's a long story I can tell you tomorrow. But aside from that, I'm his wife's secret sister. Even if Joel did like me, he'd surely regret being involved with me, because one day he'd realize I'm a sorry substitute."

Mom sputtered. "Don't talk about yourself like that."

"I don't mean it as a reflection on me, Mom. I mean Adriana had as sterling a reputation in town as Doug does. She was special."

"Well, so are you. Besides, how do you know Joel doesn't like you?"

"Mom, please." She took a drink, grateful for the excuse to look away.

"I'm serious. How do you know he'd regret being with you? Because last I checked, only God knows what the future holds, sweetheart."

"Yes, of course, but—"

Her mom's cell phone pinged from its spot on the love seat cushion. "Sorry. I forgot to turn off some notifications. Give me a moment to tweak my settings."

"No worries." They didn't need to finish this conversation, anyway. Harper couldn't risk opening her heart any further to Joel. That road only led to hurt, and it was just best if she left town.

"Yikes, I have a lot more emails than I expected." Mom scrolled through her phone. "Here's one from Joel. I didn't expect to hear from him so soon."

Would her heart always thump like this at the sound of his name? "Is he scheduling an appointment with you?"

"Yes, there's a list of times he's free for us to talk this week about the estate, and an apology about what happened with him transposing the numbers in our address, and—"

"What?"

"Listen to this. *Please accept my sincerest apologies for mixing up numbers in your address and thinking the worst. My error caused an unforgivable delay in you learning of your father's passing, but the conclusions I jumped to grieve me…*" Mom looked up. "Not a lot of people own up to mistakes like that. He's a good guy."

"Yep."

"Oh, now he's mentioning my inheritance from Dad's estate. He wants me to have an idea of what was coming." She burst into tears. "A few boxes of my mom's things, including her photo albums. I didn't realize until after I ran away that I had nothing of my mother's to re-member her by. This is such a gift."

"I can't wait to look at the photos." Shifting on the love seat, Harper hugged her mom.

It wasn't easy to hold her for long, though, because Mom shoved her phone in front of her face. "I wasn't finished."

Harper let go and pulled back, the better to focus.

A monetary figure was on the phone's screen. Not a fortune but still more than Harper had ever seen at one time. "Oh, Mom."

"I don't deserve this. I ran away from my fa-ther and—"

"And he loved you."

Mom wiped her tears. "I loved him, too. Harper, don't be like me. Stay and fight. If what you want is here, well… God brought you here, didn't He?"

"I don't want to leave you, Mom."

"We can be together anywhere, honey. It doesn't have to be Phoenix. But I've got a bee in my bonnet to do something with this money from my dad, and you need to figure out what your bee is. It just might be here."

The prickling sensation of being watched drew Harper's gaze from her mom to the trees. Beau ambled in his bird way out from behind her parked car, his head swiveling on his long neck, black eyes blinking at her.

"Hello, Beau. Looking for bugs for supper?"

Mom leaned forward, her damp cheeks rounding as she smiled. "You're such a pretty boy. Why don't you have a lady friend, you handsome fellow?"

"He's alone for one reason or another." *Like me.*

Did Beau mind these solitary jaunts? Was he an adventurer, or was he looking for something?

I came here looking for something, Lord. My father. But You had so much more for me here—

Beau interrupted her prayer with three short cries. Then the green base of his tail train rose, the hue shifting to golden bronze in the summer-evening light as the eye-spotted tail feathers unfurled into a semicircle of iridescent blues and greens. To Harper's surprise, he shook his blue body, and the stunning plumage quivered like leaves in a stiff wind, making a rattling noise. He turned slowly, as if giving them ample opportunity to admire his beauty from all angles.

They did, wordless, with Mom snapping a few photos on her phone. Then Beau strutted away from them, moving into the grove.

Harper was about to speak, but movement coming from behind her car caught her eye.

She put her hand on her mom's arm, forestalling her from making sudden moves or noises, and then pointed at the driveway.

A smaller, duller version of Beau stepped out, following him. Where his chest was blue, hers was creamy. She was brown where he was black, gray where he was green. But she was, in every way, as beautiful as the male of her species.

"A peahen," Mom whispered.

They watched the female follow Beau into the trees, and after a minute, his tail feathers folded back into the long train that swept behind him like a royal cape.

"What a show." Mom clapped lightly. "I thought you said he was a loner."

"He was." It was a sweet moment to witness. Unexpected. Unpredictable. And one might even say inspiring.

Because the birds had found a home here, thrived in an unexpected place and become a blessing. Had she ever thought of herself that way? As someone transplanted for a purpose to bless wherever God led her?

Watching the birds peck and step their way through the grove, Harper grinned.

"You look happy." Her mom nudged her in the ribs.

"Hopeful." She looked around, soaking in the

sights and sounds of the grove—the birds, the warm breeze in the trees and the lay of the land. "Let's go inside and scoop up some ice cream. I've got a new bee in my bonnet."

Almost a week had passed, and Joel hadn't heard a word from Harper. Sheila had confirmed receipt of his email, but she didn't set up an appointment time. She was occupied at present, she'd said, but she would be in touch.

He'd planned to catch Harper at church on Sunday. She hadn't been there, though. Maude—who, of course, knew everything—informed him they'd come to the earlier service. Something about Sheila being on European time and out of sorts.

He could understand that. He also remembered his promise to be a better friend to Maude, and he took the opportunity to hug her and invite her over to dinner later in the week. He hadn't done well checking in on her, which Adriana would have wanted.

He decided Harper probably needed space, so he didn't reach out. He had appointments early in the week, so he didn't pick up Maisie from cooking classes, but he listened to the tidbits he gleaned from Maisie and Trish about Harper.

She was on his mind as much as the custody issue was, and he wished he could talk about it with her. Wished he could talk more about Doug being her dad. Trish had noticed his preoccupation, but when she asked him about it, she chalked it up to his concern over Maisie's custody, for which Joel was grateful. He wasn't free to talk about Harper's secret.

Nor did he want to face his own. He'd come to realize he cared for Harper. Could fall for her, easier than breathing. But what a painful realization. He wasn't free to be with anyone until the custody battle was over, and Harper was—well, she was leaving town. Not to mention she was his wife's half sister.

He'd always thought she reminded him of Clark. Was there more to it than that? Had he seen Adriana in her?

He truly didn't think so, but he wrestled with it in prayer.

Thursday, he sat at his desk at the law office and checked his email one last time before he left to get Maisie from cooking class.

Three emails awaited his attention. An advertisement, a document from the county pertaining to one of the adoption cases he was working on and—his heart jumped into his throat—Larry, Sebastian's lawyer. Joel clicked harder than necessary to open the email.

Tomorrow, my client Sebastian Green will withdraw his petition for full custody of MAISIE

JANE DAVIS, a minor… There it was, in black and white. Sebastian was dropping the suit. Not only that, but he would also sign over parental rights to Joel, having decided that he *is not prepared to be a parent now or in the near future*…

There were no reasons given. Joel didn't expect any put into writing, but he had a few hunches. He'd convinced Sebastian that if they went before a judge, his gambling issues would be exposed, making it extremely unlikely he'd win custody of Maisie and access to her money—especially considering he'd abandoned Maisie and Adriana years ago. It wasn't worth paying Larry to fight a losing case.

But also, Joel had a feeling Sebastian was putting Maisie first. He'd seemed genuinely shocked by some of the responsibilities involved in taking on a child—things like doctor appointments.

But also, maybe when Maisie had fallen, Sebastian realized he wasn't the one she called for…and he didn't want to be, either.

There was nothing in the email about Joel's offer to pay for treatment for Sebastian's issues with gambling or alcohol, but Joel prayed he'd get help someday. And Joel meant what he'd said. Life with God would prove much more satisfying than any gaming app or drink.

Joel had been wrong not to pray for Sebastian, but he'd remedy that. He prayed for the man's salvation, healing and peace, as well as expressed his gratitude to God that he was going to legally be Maisie's dad.

His whoop filled the empty office.

In less than ten minutes, he was parking in front of The Olive Tree to pick up Maisie. He couldn't wait to tell Trish and Harper about Sebastian dropping the suit, but he had to be judicious. He didn't want to say anything to Maisie until they had an official court date. He could text those who'd been praying, though. Grinning, he pulled open the door to Trish's shop.

Walking inside, he almost tripped over his own feet to see Marigold and Rex instructing the kids instead of Harper.

He sidled alongside Trish, who was counting jars of honey. "Where's Harper?"

"Hello to you, too, Joel." She scrawled something in a three-ring binder. "You're usually much better mannered."

"Sorry," he said through gritted teeth. "I'm just surprised she's not here. I wanted to talk to her."

"She took some time off. She and her mother flew to Arizona yesterday afternoon. I thought you knew."

"No. Not a word."

They'd flown, though, so she hadn't taken

her car. That meant she was coming back for it…unless she'd decided that unreliable car of hers wouldn't make the drive and abandoned it.

Panic pounded through his veins. "When are they coming back?"

"I'm not sure. This is the last day of the kids' cooking classes, so she's no longer working here. She hated to miss the last day, but she said it was important. She preplanned the lesson, printed out instructions and shopped for the ingredients and everything. She's the one who found replacements in Marigold and Rex. They're doing an excellent job. Asked to be paid in snacks." She smiled at the retired couple.

"What was so important that she left without saying goodbye, though? Maisie will be devastated."

"There was a sense of urgency about the whole thing. Something must have come up in Arizona. She and her mom have been away from their home for weeks now, and I'm sure there are things that need attending to." She pushed her horn-rimmed glasses farther up her nose. "I'm sure she'll be back, though. To say goodbye and, of course, there's the grove to consider."

He glanced at Maisie, who was far enough away that she couldn't overhear him. "She told me she was going to sell it."

"Oh." Trish bit her lip. "That changes things, but I have a hard time believing she wouldn't say goodbye to us first."

Joel wasn't so sure. Harper was struggling with a lot. He could text her, but what point would it serve? She was telling him, clearly as she could, that Widow's Peak Creek was not her home.

"I am not a four-eyes, so stop saying I am."

Joel's head snapped back at the polite but loud voice of his daughter. Maisie had her hands on her hips, her chin tilted up defiantly, as she faced a pair of taller girls.

"I didn't call you that," one said, flipping her hair.

"Yes, you did, Dalia, about ten times. You, too, Britt, and I'm asking you to knock it off. Politely, because I'm not a bully."

"You couldn't bully anyone if you tried, you twig," the other girl barked.

That did it. No one talked to his daughter that way.

Trish's hand forestalled Joel. "Maisie doesn't need rescuing. Look at her. But this is my store, my class, and Harper warned me those girls might require watching. It's time for *me* to get involved."

Standing still while Trish walked across the store to confront the older girls was gut-wrenching. Joel should be the one protecting Maisie.

But then Joel looked at his daughter. Really looked at her.

Her chin was up at a confident angle. Her eyes were clear, dry of tears. She wasn't self-conscious, as she used to be about her eyeglasses.

Nor was she smug or triumphant when Trish doled out the discipline to the older girls, insisting they apologize and warning that they wouldn't be welcome back to future classes if anything like this ever happened again.

Maisie turned back to Nora and picked up what looked like a citrus zester. In seconds, she was grating lemon peel over the contents of her bowl like a pro.

His fragile little girl…wasn't so fragile anymore. She might be smaller than average, but that didn't mean she wasn't mighty.

A wave of love and gratitude washed over him. It was hard not to gush over her when she was finished with her class and offered him a taste of her fruit ices.

"Watermelon, berry and lemon ices. They're healthy." She pointed to the three scoops in her paper bowl.

"They look good, Bug."

"The watermelon is watery, but it's a pretty color."

"Watermelon is kind of watery anyway, but

it's refreshing on a hot day." He dug the plastic spoon into the reddish ice and tasted it. "Great work."

"Yeah, I do all right in the kitchen." Her casual shrug made him smile.

Much as he wanted to talk to Trish about Larry's email, she was busy, so he'd tell her later. After thanking her, Marigold and Rex, Joel and Maisie walked out to the truck. "Speaking of doing all right," he said once they were buckled into their seats, "I couldn't help but hear you with those older girls. You were amazing. But are you okay?"

"My feelings used to be hurt when they called me a shrimp or made fun of my glasses—but Harper said God's children are like fancy paintings in a museum, and you don't let anyone park your car on top of a fancy painting. So I used my voice and said no."

"Harper said that?"

"Yeah. And that I'm a beautiful masterpiece. I mean, Dalia and Britt are, too, but they aren't acting like it, so I feel sorry for them."

"You never told me they were giving you problems."

"I never told anybody."

"Harper knew."

"She guessed, but she didn't know for sure because Dalia and Britt lied to her. But she talked to me just in case. Later, I'll tell her what I did."

"She'll be proud, honey."

If she ever came back.

On the way home, as he drove past her property, he stared through the trees, but there was no movement. He didn't even see Beau.

Over the next few days, he told his friends about Sebastian dropping the suit, and they joined him in celebrating and thanking God. Happy as he was, his emotions were tempered by his newly strained relationship with Doug and Harper's abrupt departure. He'd confronted Doug and got the cold shoulder as a result, and he wasn't sure where to go from here. Doug was still Maisie's grandfather, and he wanted to keep a relationship for her sake. But how was he supposed to relate to Doug when he was so angry at him?

Pray. The answer was obvious, and it was the best course to follow when it came to Harper, too.

Talking with God, he realized a few things about himself that he didn't like—ways he'd erred—but he also gained perspective.

He needed to talk to Harper, to make things right and tell her about Sebastian's choice to withdraw his petition for custody. He almost texted her but decided to wait. If she wasn't back by Monday, he'd get in touch.

Every hour that passed without her made him antsy, though, and on Saturday, he was not in the proper attitude for the Good Shepherd picnic. Sure, it would be a good time of fellowship, not to mention the tri-tip on the barbecue. The mouthwatering aroma of the beef carried on the breeze and made his stomach growl.

But his heart wasn't in it.

"Look how many people are here," Trish marveled as they arrived at Hughes Park. "I think the whole church came."

"A bunch of people are in a big cluster." Maisie sounded panicked. "I hope the games didn't start without us."

"I'm sure they haven't, Bug. People are talking, that's all." He made out Marigold, Maude, Clementine... Benton and Leah, back from their honeymoon. Ah, that was it. The group was welcoming the newlyweds back to town.

Then Clementine stepped out, revealing two women with reddish-blond hair in the center of the group. Harper and Sheila.

"Harper!" Maisie's shout turned Harper around, and with a huge grin, she opened her arms. Maisie ran into them.

"Look who's back." Trish nudged his arm.

But for how long?

Joel couldn't just let her go again. Not without speaking his peace.

* * *

Harper squeezed Maisie tightly. "I'm sorry I didn't say goodbye before my quick trip."

"I knew you'd be back." Maisie pulled back. "We can cook later, right?"

"Right." Much as she wanted to introduce Maisie to her mother, there'd be time for that later. Right now, her mom was locked in a long, warm embrace with Rowena, and Maisie was practically bouncing, as if she were already in the inflatable house set up by the grill. "Where's your dad?"

Maisie shrugged. "Around here somewhere. I'm going to the bounce house, okay?"

"Okay." There was already a group of children in there, laughing and shrieking.

Joel might be nowhere in sight, but Trish was mere yards away.

God, please grant me courage. Harper walked toward Trish as a flutter of nerves shimmied in her stomach.

"Trish, there's something I need to tell you. Later this evening, or tomorrow, could we find a time to talk?"

With a sad smile, Trish touched Harper's elbow. "Is this about the fact you're my niece?"

Harper's jaw came unhinged. At last, she found words. "Joel told you?"

"Not a word." Trish's eyes were sad. "I received a notification from the genealogy website that I had a genetic match. Naturally, I clicked the link, and there was your name."

Of course. If Harper had been shown the names of people with whom she shared DNA, it made sense that they'd learn of her existence, too. "Why didn't you say anything?"

"Once I got over the initial shock that you were Doug's child—I had no idea, and I have a bone to pick with my brother—I realized what a shock it must've been to you, too. You needed to handle it in your own way. I hoped one day you'd be ready to talk, though, so I could do this." Trish wrapped her arms around Harper, clinging tightly.

Tears stung Harper's eyes as she clung back. "I'm so glad God brought you to Widow's Peak Creek. I'm so glad you're my family."

A sob escaped Harper. She couldn't help it. The only family she'd ever known was her mother, and beyond that, she'd felt unwanted. Unneeded, unnoticed.

But not anymore. Now she had two family members who loved her and whom she loved. "Thank you, Trish. I'm so blessed to have you for an aunt, and to be an aunt to Maisie."

"Don't forget Joel. I think he wants a word with you."

Harper turned and there he was, waiting. Her knees went weak just looking at him.

When she'd left with her mom on Sunday, she prayed her feelings for him would fade at the town boundary, but instead, they'd only grown. Would it ever stop, this ache of wanting to be with him?

Praying now for calm, she gave Trish a final hug and moved to join Joel.

His eyes focused on hers. "I wasn't sure when we'd see you again."

"I'm sorry I left without saying goodbye. We wanted to handle some things as quickly as possible."

"Is everything all right in Arizona?"

"Completely. We had to pack some things and schedule the move, though."

"You're moving." His eyes narrowed a fraction.

"Here. To Widow's Peak Creek."

He didn't speak. Didn't smile or frown or give her any clue what he was thinking. Then he reached for her hand. "Come here."

She had no idea what he planned to say, but the bones in her hand felt like melted butter.

He led her away from the others, their path curving around the large boulder that jutted out into the creek. It was slightly more private here, considering they were surrounded by people, but they were out of the line of their friends' and families' sight, and the rushing of the water around the boulder gave them the freedom to speak without worrying if they were overheard.

"Tell me more about moving here." Joel leaned his shoulder against the boulder.

She copied his posture, resting her hip against the cool granite. "My mom has always wanted to help young people the way she was helped when she needed a hand. So we're combining our inheritances from Clark to start a business. Pavone Grove—*pavone* is Italian for *peacock*. We're talking to an artist about getting an illustration of Beau for the oil labels. Oh, I forgot to tell you, he has a peahen friend. I hope they come back soon so Maisie can see them."

"Hold up. Oil labels?"

"Yes, did I forget to say that? We'll be bottling and selling olive oils. Everything the grove-management company does now, we're going to learn to do for ourselves and then teach young people. Mom is attending 'olive school' starting next week. In the meantime, we'll fix up the barn. It'll be the center of operations when it comes to bottling, labeling and shipping oils. We're going to sell them locally as well as online."

"That's amazing."

"The work is seasonal, but hopefully it will give some young people skills and job experience—and maybe even pay for itself so it's not all funded by my mother's inheritance. But it's such a blessing to have it so we can get this off the ground."

"I can recommend a lawyer if you need one."

"Hey, you do family law," she teased.

"I meant a friend who does business law, but I know my way around a contract. And I don't require payment, although baklava is always welcome." His eyes grew serious. "What about your work as a pastry chef?"

"I got a call from the Greek deli in town wanting desserts. Maybe more restaurants will follow. I can work from home while Pavone gets off the ground. Then we'll see what God has in store."

"You're staying in Widow's Peak Creek. For good." His full lips curved into a wide, happy smile. "There was a day when that would have surprised me."

"Me too. I never expected to fall in love with this town, but I did. And its people. Maisie. And—"

She broke off, swallowing hard. "I always wanted to know who my dad was, but when I learned it was Doug, it was awful. But God redeemed it, in a way. If Doug weren't my dad, I wouldn't be related to Trish or Maisie. Blood doesn't always make a family—I know that—but in this case?"

"It's pretty significant." His small smile looked sad. "After you left, I confronted Doug on his poor treatment of you and your mom, then and now. I wish I could say he was repentant, but the truth is, I don't know if he'll ever respond to you the way you deserve. The facade he presented of a generous, friendly man never penetrated to his heart, and who he is—someone who'd turn his back on his child and her mother to protect his reputation and money—has made me angry and sad. I feel I need to keep a relationship with him for Maisie's sake but don't want you to think I'm okay with what he did. I'll never be okay with it, the way he's hurt you."

"*Hurt* doesn't begin to describe how I feel, but God has gifted me with pity for him. He's chosen to prioritize all the wrong things, so I'm glad you're still in his life. He needs love, even the tough variety. Next time you speak to him alone, please assure him I won't spill his secrets. No one will ever find out he's my father from me."

"I've had enough of secrets for a lifetime."

"Then I need to tell you something else since I'm staying in town, because it could get awkward and I want you to know why. One last secret I've been keeping." Her heart fluttered like a caged bird. "I'm in love with you. Even though—"

"I love you, too." His words both thrilled and terrified her. "Even though what?"

How could he even ask? "There's no way we can be together."

"Why not?"

How could he even ask *that*? "Because your wife was my sister. I wish I'd known who I was a lot earlier so I could've stopped myself from falling for you. And so you'd know why you felt something for me. It's because I remind you of her. You always said I was familiar."

"Because of Clark, another person I loved. Not because of Adriana."

"Okay, but someday you'd realize you settled for second-best. The rejected little sister. This all could've been avoided if only I'd known who I was."

"At the pizza parlor, you said 'I want to know who I am.' Well, I'll tell you who I think you are, and it doesn't have to do with your biological father." His eyes blazed. "You're the woman whose smile makes my stomach do summersaults. The woman whose love for God shines from her eyes and whose affection for Maisie makes my heart feel like it's going to explode. You should've seen her this past week, standing up to these girls who've been making things hard for her. She had confidence because of the words you shared with her."

"She did?"

"She did." Joel took her hand in both of his.

"You're good for her. You're good for both of us, and when you left, it was like the sun went dark on me. It's because I love you. I loved you before I knew Doug was your dad. I didn't love you because you reminded me of anyone. I loved you because of who you are, in your heart and mind, and I'm never going to get over it."

Thrilling as his words were, they didn't change anything. "We still can't be together. I don't want to contribute to anything that Sebastian's attorney could use against you. I won't jeopardize your chances for custody."

Joel winced. "I'm sorry I didn't defend you when the attorney brought you and your mom into the conversation. Your mom isn't part of this, and you've done nothing but care for Maisie. I'm also sorry for letting his manipulation dictate how I treated you. I should have told you why I was reluctant to let you watch Maisie. I shouldn't have hesitated to offer you a ride to Benton and Leah's wedding when Beau was on the car, but I didn't want to fuel rumors. I told myself I was protecting Maisie, but I realize now that I was a coward."

Coward? "No, Joel."

"Yes. I was wrong to care so much about what others thought, to make choices based on fear."

"I get it, though. I'd be scared of losing Maisie, too."

"But I should have trusted God, should've fought for her knowing He was in charge, and I had nothing to hide. I still don't. The past few days, I've had some long conversations with God. I've seen how mistaken I've been, especially with you. It sent me to my knees in shame, but I was reading a Psalm where the author compared himself to a green olive tree in God's house. It caught my attention because you and olives will forever go together with me—but I also realized it's a fruitful, useful tree. The author used it for the comparison not just because of that, though, but because of where it was planted. It was rooted in God."

He squeezed her hand between his warm ones. "I realized that I'm going to make mistakes, but if I'm rooted in Christ, I'll be growing in Him. So while I can't promise perfection, I can promise I want to be a better man. For Him. For Maisie. For you." He took a deep breath. "You should never be anyone's secret. Not as a daughter and not as the woman I love. I want to shout it to the whole world, Harper. I only hope you can forgive me."

She'd waited so long to hear words like this from the man she loved, but her heart ached within her chest. "There's nothing to forgive. I'm growing, too. I don't think we ever stop growing—at least, I hope we don't. But I still think it might be best if you focused on the adoption. Maisie is most important."

"Your consideration is one of the things I love about you, but it's not necessary in this situation. Sebastian dropped his suit."

"What?" Words she'd prayed to hear. "When?"

"A few days ago. I think he realized parenting was a lot more involved than he expected."

"Praise God. So the adoption is on?" At his happy nod, she almost cried. "That's wonderful, but…what if anyone finds out about Doug being my dad? It'll shock people, for sure."

"If folks choose to gossip, it's between them and God. But I imagine there's already talk spreading about us." His gaze settled on her mouth. "The whole church saw us go behind this rock. Me marrying you is going to be the least shocking thing to happen in Widow's Peak Creek since the sun rose this morning."

Hold up. "We're getting married?"

He placed her hand on his pounding heart. There was no artifice there. No beating out that she was second-best. Only love.

So when he lowered his head and kissed her, her hand left his heart and curled behind his neck, pulling him closer. She forgot where she was, and she wasn't just weak-kneed by his kiss—she was practically boneless.

"Marry me?" His whisper fanned her cheek.

"I want to spend my whole life proclaiming my love for you, in word and deed."

"Yes." Her heart was pattering a hundred times a minute.

"Hey," a high-pitched voice yelled. "Does this mean I get to be in another wedding?"

Laughing, Harper opened her arms to Maisie. "Yes!"

Joel wrapped his arms around both of them. He was smiling when he kissed Harper this time, and she probably was, too. She'd never known such happiness.

And she would never take a single moment of it for granted.

Epilogue

December 21

"Put on your coat, Maisie. It's cool enough to snow tonight." Harper held out the crimson jacket for Maisie as they stood in the grand foyer of Hughes House, the town museum, during the annual Gingerbread Gala. Her lips twitched because even though it didn't snow in Widow's Peak Creek, they were expecting quite a blizzard tonight.

Of fake snow, that is.

"I was here last year." Maisie donned her jacket quickly. "I'm not supposed to ruin the secret for anyone, but the 'snow' is really bubbles."

Harper had figured that out when she looked outside and recognized the tall apparatus that sent "flakes" of white flittering to the ground. "I won't spoil the surprise."

"See you." Maisie ran off to join the other children in the backyard. A sense of expectation filled the winter evening, and Harper shivered as she grabbed her own coat from the hook, a sleek-cut tartan pattern that complemented her Christmas-green dress.

"Allow me." Joel appeared at her elbow to help her with her coat.

"Hey, lovebirds, use it or lose it." Maude pointed at the mistletoe hanging from the chandelier above them.

"I say 'use it.' It's tradition, after all." Joel gave her a brief but toe-curling kiss before making way for Maude and her new beau, Fergus, to step beneath the mistletoe. Fergus smooched Maude's cheek, and she giggled.

They strolled outside onto the grass between lanterns and dazzling holiday-light displays. Harper stopped to greet friends, pausing to admire Faith Santos's newborn son, Gabriel. Her heart panged with maternal longing, and she prayed she and Joel would be blessed with children of their own once they married. Regardless, they had Maisie, and they'd started talking about Harper adopting her, too. Harper automatically led Joel closer to where Maisie played on the lawn.

It was hard to believe it was Christmas already. In the past few months, there had been many changes to their lives. Joel's adoption of Maisie. Harper's blossoming career as several restaurants in town served her desserts. Plus all the activity at the grove. The old barn now housed an office and equipment, and just before the olives ripened to a dark purple-black, Sheila hired several young adults who'd recently aged out of the foster care system. They harvested the crop, and within days of bottling the first of the oil, they'd made their first local sales…and were greeted by Beau, the peahen they'd named Bella, and their troop of fuzzy yellow-brown peafowl chicks.

Harper hoped the birds were safe and warm tonight as the chill nipped her cheeks and ears. Then, against the dark winter sky, the "snow" started, and the crowd *ooh*ed and *ahh*ed as the snow, artificial but beautiful, fell from overhead. Sheila and Maisie held out their hands to catch the snow. Beside them, Trish and her "gentleman caller" Harvey looked on with amusement.

Nothing had changed with Doug, despite Trish's and Joel's attempts that he acknowledge Harper in some way. But Harper hadn't stopped praying for him. She found peace in knowing who she was now—not because she knew her father's identity but because she was God's child.

The Christmas lights caught on her engagement ring, making the stone flash like fire. She looked up at Joel. "Let's get married."

"I already thought we were." He stood behind her and wrapped his arms around her, drawing her against him to enjoy the sight of children frolicking in the bubble snow.

"I mean sooner than planned. By New Year's, even."

"But the house isn't ready."

They'd decided to build a bigger house on the bare plot at the grove, but construction had barely started.

"I don't care where we live. If you don't mind marrying soon, that is."

He answered by kissing her in front of everyone, warming her to her toes.

God had blessed her with more than she could ever have imagined when she arrived in Widow's Peak Creek: family, friends and a future with this man and his daughter.

She was ready to start living it.

* * * * *

If you enjoyed this story, look for these other books by Susanne Dietze:

A Future for His Twins
Seeking Sanctuary
A Small-Town Christmas Challenge
A Need to Protect

Dear Reader,

While researching an earlier book in the Widow's Peak Creek series, I learned some of the forty-niners who came to California in the mid-1800s planted olive trees, many of which are still producing today. I just had to set a story in a grove with old trees. As for the mishap with Joel's letters, something similar happened to me. I once sent a Christmas card that took months to arrive at its destination because I had mixed up two numbers in the address. Now I am very careful when addressing envelopes!

I hope you've enjoyed Joel and Harper's story as they learned to trust God with their futures. Theirs is the final tale in the Widow's Peak Creek series. The characters have become friends to me, and they will live on my heart and imagination for years to come. But for now, I'm working hard on something new. Stay tuned!

In the meantime, you can find me online at my website, www.susannedietze.com, with links to my newsletter and social media accounts.

Thank you for supporting Christian fiction

and allowing me the opportunity to share my stories. I'm grateful to you, from the bottom of my heart.

Blessings,
Susanne

Get 4 FREE REWARDS!

We'll send you 2 FREE Books plus 2 FREE Mystery Gifts.

FREE
Value Over
$20

Both the **Love Inspired®** and **Love Inspired®** Suspense series feature compelling novels filled with inspirational romance, faith, forgiveness, and hope.

YES! Please send me 2 FREE novels from the Love Inspired or Love Inspired Suspense series and my 2 FREE gifts (gifts are worth about $10 retail). After receiving them, if I don't wish to receive any more books, I can return the shipping statement marked "cancel." If I don't cancel, I will receive 6 brand-new Love Inspired Larger-Print books or Love Inspired Suspense Larger-Print books every month and be billed just $5.99 each in the U.S. or $6.24 each in Canada. That is a savings of at least 17% off the cover price. It's quite a bargain! Shipping and handling is just 50¢ per book in the U.S. and $1.25 per book in Canada.* I understand that accepting the 2 free books and gifts places me under no obligation to buy anything. I can always return a shipment and cancel at any time. The free books and gifts are mine to keep no matter what I decide.

Choose one: ☐ **Love Inspired**
Larger-Print
(122/322 IDN GNWC)

☐ **Love Inspired Suspense**
Larger-Print
(107/307 IDN GNWN)

Name (please print)

Address   Apt. #

City   State/Province   Zip/Postal Code

Email: Please check this box ☐ if you would like to receive newsletters and promotional emails from Harlequin Enterprises ULC and its affiliates. You can unsubscribe anytime.

Mail to the Harlequin Reader Service:
IN U.S.A.: P.O. Box 1341, Buffalo, NY 14240-8531
IN CANADA: P.O. Box 603, Fort Erie, Ontario L2A 5X3

Want to try 2 free books from another series? Call 1-800-873-8635 or visit www.ReaderService.com.

*Terms and prices subject to change without notice. Prices do not include sales taxes, which will be charged (if applicable) based on your state or country of residence. Canadian residents will be charged applicable taxes. Offer not valid in Quebec. This offer is limited to one order per household. Books received may not be as shown. Not valid for current subscribers to the Love Inspired or Love Inspired Suspense series. All orders subject to approval. Credit or debit balances in a customer's account(s) may be offset by any other outstanding balance owed by or to the customer. Please allow 4 to 6 weeks for delivery. Offer available while quantities last.

Your Privacy—Your information is being collected by Harlequin Enterprises ULC, operating as Harlequin Reader Service. For a complete summary of the information we collect, how we use this information and to whom it is disclosed, please visit our privacy notice located at corporate.harlequin.com/privacy-notice. From time to time we may also exchange your personal information with reputable third parties. If you wish to opt out of this sharing of your personal information, please visit readerservice.com/consumerchoice or call 1-800-873-8635. **Notice to California Residents**—Under California law, you have specific rights to control and access your data. For more information on these rights and how to exercise them, visit corporate.harlequin.com/california-privacy.

LIRLIS22

Get 4 FREE REWARDS!

We'll send you 2 FREE Books plus 2 FREE Mystery Gifts.

FREE Value Over **$20**

Both the **Harlequin® Special Edition** and **Harlequin® Heartwarming™** series feature compelling novels filled with stories of love and strength where the bonds of friendship, family and community unite.

YES! Please send me 2 FREE novels from the Harlequin Special Edition or Harlequin Heartwarming series and my 2 FREE gifts (gifts are worth about $10 retail). After receiving them, if I don't wish to receive any more books, I can return the shipping statement marked "cancel." If I don't cancel, I will receive 6 brand-new Harlequin Special Edition books every month and be billed just $4.99 each in the U.S or $5.74 each in Canada, a savings of at least 17% off the cover price or 4 brand-new Harlequin Heartwarming Larger-Print books every month and be billed just $5.74 each in the U.S. or $6.24 each in Canada, a savings of at least 21% off the cover price. It's quite a bargain! Shipping and handling is just 50¢ per book in the U.S. and $1.25 per book in Canada.* I understand that accepting the 2 free books and gifts places me under no obligation to buy anything. I can always return a shipment and cancel at any time. The free books and gifts are mine to keep no matter what I decide.

Choose one: ☐ **Harlequin Special Edition** ☐ **Harlequin Heartwarming**
(235/335 HDN GNMP)   **Larger-Print**
(161/361 HDN GNPZ)

Name (please print)

Address   Apt. #

City   State/Province   Zip/Postal Code

Email: Please check this box ☐ if you would like to receive newsletters and promotional emails from Harlequin Enterprises ULC and its affiliates. You can unsubscribe anytime.

Mail to the **Harlequin Reader Service:**
IN U.S.A.: P.O. Box 1341, Buffalo, NY 14240-8531
IN CANADA: P.O. Box 603, Fort Erie, Ontario L2A 5X3

Want to try 2 free books from another series! Call 1-800-873-8635 or visit www.ReaderService.com.

COUNTRY LEGACY COLLECTION

19 FREE BOOKS IN ALL!

Cowboys, adventure and romance await you in this new collection! Enjoy superb reading all year long with books by bestselling authors like Diana Palmer, Sasha Summers and Marie Ferrarella!

YES! Please send me the **Country Legacy Collection!** This collection begins with 3 FREE books and 2 FREE gifts in the first shipment. Along with my 3 free books, I'll also get 3 more books from the **Country Legacy Collection**, which I may either return and owe nothing or keep for the low price of $24.60 U.S./$28.12 CDN each plus $2.99 U.S./$7.49 CDN for shipping and handling per shipment*. If I decide to continue, about once a month for 8 months, I will get 6 or 7 more books but will only pay for 4. That means 2 or 3 books in every shipment will be FREE! If I decide to keep the entire collection, I'll have paid for only 32 books because 19 are FREE! I understand that accepting the 3 free books and gifts places me under no obligation to buy anything. I can always return a shipment and cancel at any time. My free books and gifts are mine to keep no matter what I decide.

☐ 275 HCK 1939   ☐ 475 HCK 1939

Name (please print)

Address   Apt. #

City   State/Province   Zip/Postal Code

Mail to the Harlequin Reader Service:
IN U.S.A.: P.O. Box 1341, Buffalo, NY 14240-8571
IN CANADA: P.O. Box 603, Fort Erie, Ontario L2A 5X3

Visit
ReaderService.com
Today!

**As a valued member of the
Harlequin Reader Service,
you'll find these benefits and more at
ReaderService.com:**

- Try 2 free books from any series
- Access risk-free special offers
- View your account history & manage payments
- Browse the latest Bonus Bucks catalog

Don't miss out!

If you want to stay up-to-date on the latest at the Harlequin Reader Service and enjoy more content, make sure you've signed up for our monthly News & Notes email newsletter. Sign up online at ReaderService.com or by calling Customer Service at 1-800-873-8635.

RS20